James T. Bixby

The Crisis in Morals

An examination of rational ethics in the light of modern science

James T. Bixby

The Crisis in Morals
 An examination of rational ethics in the light of modern science

ISBN/EAN: 9783337380915

Printed in Europe, USA, Canada, Australia, Japan

Cover: Foto ©Andreas Hilbeck / pixelio.de

More available books at **www.hansebooks.com**

THE CRISIS IN MORALS.

✠

An Examination of Rational Ethics
in the
Light of Modern Science.

✠

BY

JAMES THOMPSON BIXBY,

DOCTOR OF PHILOSOPHY OF THE UNIVERSITY OF LEIPZIG.

BOSTON:
ROBERTS BROTHERS.
1891.

University Press:

JOHN WILSON AND SON, CAMBRIDGE, U S A.

CONTENTS.

——

Part First.

CHAPTER V.

CHAPTER VI.

CHAPTER VII.

CHAPTER VIII.

CHAPTER IX.

CHAPTER X.

CHAPTER XI.

Part Second.

THE POSITIVE RECONSTRUCTION OF ETHICS ON THE BASIS OF EVOLUTION AND SCIENTIFIC KNOWLEDGE.

CHAPTER I.

CHAPTER II.

CHAPTER III.

CHAPTER IX.

CHAPTER X.

CHAPTER XI.

CHAPTER XII.

CHAPTER XIII.

CHAPTER XIV.

THE CRISIS IN MORALS.

PART I.

CRITIQUE OF HERBERT SPENCER'S "DATA OF ETHICS."

———◆———

CHAPTER I.

THE great passion of the present day is evidently the passion for reconstruction. Ancient monarchies are turned into republics, and the old heroes and patriots into demagogues or myths. What used to be reckoned sober history is now presented as a mosaic of mouldy legends or an air-castle of bold romance. The immovable earth of ancient thought has been set spinning on its axis about the sun, and the solid firmament in which it used to be thought that that sun, with the other fixed stars, were set, has been dissolved into thin air. Especially noticeable have been the changes in our ideas of creation and man's position

in the world. Instead of the six days which
it was formerly thought sufficed for the production of the various heavenly bodies and
living species, millions of years are now demanded by science, through the whole of
which the slow but ever-progressing process
of the world's unfolding is spread; and man,
instead of being considered an entirely separate order of creation, is regarded as the crown
and climax of this long development. The
success which the theory of evolution has had
in reconstructing biology, astronomy, geology,
anthropology, and even religion and philosophy,
has been remarkable. Applied by Darwin to
the origin and development of species, and by
Herbert Spencer to the explanation of the interior as well as the exterior world, it has
made new progress every day among scientific minds. It seems to become plainer and
plainer that outside this doctrine (understood in the broadest sense) there is scarce-
ly any other explanation possible for the
development of living beings than that of

miracle ; and miracle has well been called "the abdication of science."

After having so successfully transformed natural history, the temptation would be irresistible to seek the aid of the same theory to transform the history of morals and the theories of religion. A new conception of the natural world seems inevitably to involve with it a new conception of the spiritual world. In one of the most important chapters of his " Descent of Man," Charles Darwin threw out some exceedingly bold and ingenious speculations upon the origin of the moral sense. This, in his view, is a natural development from the social instincts which must have been acquired by man in a very rude state, and which probably existed even among his early ape-like progenitors.

" The more enduring social instincts," says Darwin, " conquer the less persistent instincts. After having yielded to some temptation, we feel a sense of dissatisfaction analogous to that felt from other unsatisfied instincts,

called in this case 'conscience,' for we cannot
prevent past images and impressions continually passing through our minds; and these,
in their weakened state, we compare with
the ever-present social instincts, or with habits gained in early youth and strengthened
during our whole lives, perhaps inherited,
so that they are at last rendered almost as
strong as instincts." [1]

It is this contrast of the weaker memory
of a past selfish impulse with the present
feeling of our more enduring instincts that
constitutes conscience. Remorse is only regret of unusual intensity for past imprudence.
"The imperious word 'ought,'" says Darwin,
"seems merely to imply the consciousness of
the existence of a persistent instinct, either
innate or partly acquired, serving him as a
guide, though liable to be disobeyed." And
he compares the moral sense to the instinct
of pointers to point, hounds to hunt, and re-
trievers to retrieve, who seem to him to have

---

[1] Descent of Man, i. 100.

about as much of a duty to follow out their inherited impulses as man has to follow his conscience.[1]

It was only natural that such adventurous theories, presented by the distinguished apostle of the doctrine of Natural Selection, should foster in the whole Darwinian school and its allies the most revolutionary views of the nature of morality. The problem of ethics, it was believed, could be solved at once by a thorough-going application of the laws of physics. As in the animal domain everything is derived without any miraculous intervention from one single principle (namely, the struggle for existence), so in the domain of humanity and its moral life everything is explained by a similar single, all-sufficient principle, — the gravitation of each individual or each tribe toward its own advantage. Under the power of self-love, man seeks his happiness and follows his instincts as inevitably as a stone falls to the ground.

[1] Descent of Man, p. 87.

The cosmogony of Hesiod, with its successive creations and generations of gods, seems no more fabulous to the Darwinians than that moral cosmogony which attributes to a supernatural principle the laws of the moral world. The time-honored principles of ethics that recognized the moral sense as innate, the verdicts of conscience as authoritative, and the sanctions of morality as God-given, are daily discredited.

Mr. John Morley, in his work on "Compromise," bluntly tells us that "moral principles, where they are true, are only registered generalizations from experience. . . . A natural right is a mere figment of the imagination. . . . The only reason for recognizing any supposed right or claim inherent in any man or body of men, other than what is expressly conferred by positive law, ever has been and still is general utility."

And Matthew Arnold echoes this by adopting as his own the doctrine that "All rights are created by law and are based on expediency, and are alterable as the public advantage may require." [1]

An American pioneer in this work of moral reconstruction on the new basis of expediency is still more thoroughgoing. "Moral rules," says Mr. Van Buren Denslow, in his work entitled "Modern Thinkers," which Mr. Robert Ingersoll considered worthy of the honor of an introduction from his brilliant pen, "are doctrines established by the strong for the government of the weak." In Mr. Denslow's view, the commandments against theft, lying, unchastity, and so on, are the cords by which the property owners and the successful ones in the struggle for existence would hold down more securely those over whom they have got the advantage. The prompting to steal and lie is as much a prompting of nature with the weak as the commandments prohibiting these acts are naturally urged on the weak by the stronger ones who wish to keep the weak in subjection. They are not universal but class

[1] Fortnightly Review, New Series, vol. xxiii. p. 317.

laws. "Philosophy," Mr. Denslow declares, "will see in this contest of antagonistic forces a mere play of opposing elements, in which larceny is an incident of social weakness and unfitness to survive, just as debility and leprosy are. I would as soon assume a divine command, 'Thou shalt not break out in boils and sores,' to the weakling or leper, as one of 'Thou shalt not steal,' to the failing struggler for subsistence."[1]

Few of these modern essays at the transmutation of morals are as radical as this. But any one who is familiar with such recent works in this field as M. Guyau's "Esquisse d'une Morale sans Obligation ni Sanction," Gizycki's "Manual of Ethical Philosophy," Mr. Cotter Morison's "Service of Man," or Mr. Wordsworth Donisthorpe's recent work entitled "Individualism," cannot fail to see that we have come to a momentous crisis in the conception and treatment of morals. The immense success of the theory of evolution has thoroughly

[1] Modern Thinkers, p. 245.

unsettled the views of the younger generation and made them suspect the old foundations.

Undoubtedly they need to be examined. And it is well to have any new theories that have a show of good evidence brought up and compared with them. It is the purpose of this book to submit to a careful examination the new theories of ethics which the modern evolution philosophy has given rise to; and I have selected for this purpose the work of him whom Charles Darwin most properly called "our great philosopher." Certainly among the great thinkers of the last half of the nineteenth century there is none whose work has been more epoch-making than that of Herbert Spencer. If Charles Darwin himself, by his masterly scientific researches upon natural selection, laid the corner-stone of the modern theory of evolution, certainly it was Herbert Spencer's comprehensive exposition of the synthetic philosophy, as he preferred to call it, and his brilliant and elaborate presentation of those principles in biology, psychology, sociology,

religion, and ethics that (more than any other
one man's efforts) gave the evolution theory
its present completeness, persuasiveness, and
public acceptance. The evidence accumulated
in its favor from hundreds of different quarters,
although not amounting to positive demonstra-
tion, is yet so extensive and varied as to make
intelligent minds accept it as the most probable
theory. While there are many points in Mr.
Spencer's synthetic philosophy from which I
entirely dissent, it is undoubtedly full of
acute argumentation and luminous explanations. It contains many brilliant and valuable
expositions, which have thrown new light upon
the laws of life, of consciousness, and of social
growth. It was only natural that, as the new
theories had been so successful in these
scientific domains, they should be applied to
the moral domain. They might well be expected to give us some fresh clews with which
to explore the labyrinths of ethics. Especially
did the great law of evolution, which in Mr.
Spencer's hand had cast its luminous beams

upon the problems of biology and sociology, seem likely to render good service in supplying a law, inductively determined, for the normal course of human nature and the rightful end of all actions, — a law and an end substantially the same as those which the clearest school of intuitive morals had so long ago divined. To establish the laws of right and wrong on a scientific basis would be to render the greatest service to humanity, and to require this of any philosophical system is to put it to the severest test. The synthetic philosophy would have been a column without a capital if it had not culminated in some systematic declaration of the outcome of the principles of evolution in that which is its highest field, — the motives and rules of human conduct. Mr. Spencer was wise, therefore, in deferring the second and third parts of his "Sociology" till he had given us the essential points of his principles of morality. Its publication, under the title of the "Data of Ethics," was an event of real importance in the history of the philosophy of evolution, and the book at once established its claim to be reckoned with by all who should thenceforth undertake to discuss the grounds and principles of morality.

It was with hope, then, as well as interest, that we awaited Mr. Spencer's exposition of the principles of ethics. His prestige as our most eminent champion and systematizer of the new philosophy would lend authority to his expositions, and his reputation for the industrious collection of facts and ingenious disentanglement of the laws involved in them was well earned. Mr. Spencer's previous work in this domain exhibited a moral enthusiasm and a comprehension of the shortcomings of the Utilitarian School which seemed likely to save him from its errors, while his scientific and philosophic studies would lead him to find in physical and human nature solid foundations for our motives of right and wrong which many popular representatives of the Intuitive School had overlooked.

CHAPTER II.

WHAT measure of success, then, has crowned Mr. Spencer's work in this highest domain of philosophy, this severest test of his theory?

We need only to read a little way in the "Data of Ethics" to see that Mr. Spencer here, as in his previous books, has essayed a new departure. His ethics constitute a very different system from that of Kant or the orthodox Intuitive School.

The great German philosopher, in his work on the foundations of the metaphysics of ethics, took for his starting-point the idea of good-will, seeking to find its simplest and purest state. Our English philosopher begins at the antipodal point of good *conduct,* and searches in the depths of the animal scale to find what it is in its simplest form among inferior beings. From these lowly phenomena

of well or ill evolved conduct presented by
oysters and worms, he ascends through the
various animal species to man, and through
the various stages of savage and semi-civilized
life to the ideal conduct of perfected humanity. Human conduct, he assumes, is only a
part of universal conduct; morals are only
the culminating phase of the behavior of
living beings. The essential thing in it
is the more and more perfect adaptation of
means to ends. The last stages of universal
conduct, which, by way of distinction, are
called ethical, are those "displayed by the
highest type of being where he is forced, by
increase of numbers, to live more and more
in presence of his fellows." [1]

What, then, is good conduct as distinguished
from bad ?

It is simply, in Spencer's view, that conduct
which is adapted to its end, that which is
relatively more evolved. And as evolution
tends ever toward self-preservation, it is such

[1] Data of Ethics, p. 20.

as furthers self-preservation, and next, the preservation of those who are to continue the species, and the preservation of the neighbors without whose aid our individual life cannot reach its own perfection. Conduct becomes the best when it fulfils at the same time all these three ends, — "totality of life in self, in offspring, and in fellow-men." [1] But why do we call these acts conducive to life good? Mr. Spencer does not recognize either life or perfection of being as ends sufficient in themselves. Life, in his view, is of worth only when it brings a surplus of agreeable feeling. Goodness can be ascribed to acts subserving life only, then, on the assumption that they help to produce a "surplus of pleasurable feeling over painful feeling." [2] "Acts are good or bad according as their aggregate effects increase men's happiness or increase their misery." [3] "The conception of virtue cannot

[1] Data of Ethics, p. 26. The citations from the "Data of Ethics" are made from the American edition, New York, D. Appleton & Co., 1880.

[2] Ibid., p. 30.   [3] Ibid., p. 40.

be separated from the conception of happiness-producing conduct." [1]

How, then, may we best judge of conduct? We must not rely upon a supernaturally given conscience, but we must determine the natural relations between acts and results. But for this it is not sufficient to make direct observation of the results that present themselves to us, but we must find out the general laws of life and conditions of existence, and from these fundamental principles deduce what conduct will be detrimental and what beneficial. A direct pursuit of happiness is apt to defeat its own end, since the components of happiness cannot be safely and surely calculated. Happiness cannot, then, be taken as the proximate guide of conduct. This proximate guide is found in the intuitive principles of ethics and those instinctive moral sentiments which are the products of the past experiences of utility of preceding generations, organized and consolidated within us by heredity.

[1] Data of Ethics, p. 38.

The study of evolving conduct shows that "for the better preservation of life, the primitive, simple, presentative feelings must be controlled by the later-evolved, compound, and representative feelings." [1] The reason is, that "guidance by the more complex feeling, on the average, conduces to welfare more than does guidance by the simpler feeling." [2] As life advances, the feelings become more and more ideal. "Hence it follows that as guides, the feelings have authority proportionate to the degrees in which they are removed by their complexity and their ideality from simple sensations and appetites." [3]

How, then, do our moral intuitions and sense of duty arise ? They are simply the results of accumulated experiences of the pleasures and pains of our ancestors, gradually organized, accumulated by inheritance, and transmuted into moral emotions, and which have thus come to be quite indepen-

[1] Data of Ethics, p. 113.
[2] Ibid., p. 107.   [3] Ibid., p. 109.

dent of conscious experience.[1] It has been by
the effects of punishments inflicted by law
and public opinion on conduct of certain
kinds that "the sense of compulsion which
the consciousness of duty includes, and which
the word 'obligation' indicates," is generated.[2]
The sense of duty Mr. Spencer therefore
calls an abstract idea, which disengages itself
insensibly from these coarser restraints and
acquires an "illusive independence." But this
sense of duty is transitory, and will diminish as fast as moralization increases. There
are various changing systems of ethics, two
especially, — the war-code of enmity, and the
industrial code of amity, proper to changing
ratios between warlike activities and peaceful activities; but as civilization advances,
the code of industrialism gains the predominance. Pure egoism and pure altruism are
both illegitimate. Some mixture of the two
is necessary. And to obtain the highest sum
of happiness, every man must be more ego-

[1] Data of Ethics, p. 123.   [2] Ibid., p. 126.

istic than altruistic; and while civilization demands a certain measure of altruistic activities, "the opportunities for that postponement of self to others, which constitutes altruism as ordinarily conceived, must in several ways be more and more limited as the highest state is approached." [1]

In chapter xv. Mr. Spencer passes on to a consideration of absolute ethics. He repudiates the idea that there is in every case a right and a wrong, and contends that in many cases there is only a least wrong; and in many more it is not possible to ascertain with any precision which is the least wrong. "Pain," he says, "is the correlative of some species of wrong;" and "conduct which has any concomitant of pain or any painful consequence is partially wrong." [2] The absolutely right actions are those which benefit all parties concerned, and which are merely pleasurable alike in their immediate and remote effects. Absolute ethics is the formulation

---

[1] Data of Ethics, p. 251.   [2] Ibid., p. 261.

of the ideal conduct of the ideal man who
is perfectly evolved, as he would exist in
the ideal social state. This supplies the standard which relative ethics, such as alone are
feasible at present, has to take as the standard by which to estimate divergencies from
right or degrees of wrong. After considering
this subject at some length, Mr. Spencer concludes that a code of perfect personal conduct can never be made definite, because
various types of men adapted to various
types of activities may lead lives that are
severally complete after their kind. The particular requirements of morals will vary with
variations in the natural conditions of society.
The chief function of absolute ethics is to
keep before consciousness an ideal concilia-
tion of the various claims involved, and suggest the search for such compromise among
them as shall satisfy all to the greatest
extent practicable.[1]

Such are the main points of the " Data of

[1] Data cf Ethics, chap. xvi.

Ethics." Mr. Spencer could hardly write a book upon any subject, least of all upon the principles of morality, without saying something strong and fresh and acute. "The Data of Ethics" contains not a little which is of incontestable value and importance. The author recognizes, as he says, that there is a truth in the orthodox ethical system. We can quite cordially return the compliment, and recognize a truth in his system. As a study of human behavior from the outside, ignoring the question of the motives or inner state of the subject, it shows great ingenuity, and how much more than might ever be expected has been accomplished under most hampering conditions. A most excellent point in Mr. Spencer's system is the strong infusion of the historical element found there. One of the things that we are becoming most sure of in these recent days is that nothing is to be understood by itself. Politics, society, religion, language, all have grown up to their present form from some past form.

The dictionary, the prayer-book, the manual of etiquette, are each filled with fossils, curious vestiges of ancestral life. So in tracing moral laws and forces, we find that each has had its stages of growth, and it cannot be understood as it is without knowing its history.

The attention directed by Mr. Spencer to heredity, and its influence upon ethical development, is to be commended; for it is certainly a factor which has played a most important part in strengthening the moral sense. One of the most needed elements in ethics is a proper and sufficiently binding tie between the individual man and society at large. The lack of it has led ethical theorists into all sorts of arbitrary suppositions. It drove Hobbes, for example, to resort to an imaginary " original contract," by which all men have agreed, for the sake of personal security, to transfer their natural rights to a supreme political authority; and it led Professor Bain to suppose that the

associations of a few years would account
for the harmony of feeling between the private person and the state, and that the
welfare of society might thus easily come to
be mirrored in the conscience of each individual. It is evident how much superior, both
in subtlety and in truth to the facts, is the
theory which Mr. Spencer has presented, by
which the hereditary experience of the past
is transformed into the moral instincts and
intuitions of to-day. Evolution shows that
one individual is not merely connected with
others through considerable similarity of experience, built upon an equally characterless
basis, but, as Mr. Sorley has so well ex-
pressed it, "he is organically related to all
members of the race, not only bone of their
bone and flesh of their flesh, but mind of
their mind."[1] He is connected with others by
a thousand subtly interwoven threads of emo-
tion which enter into his life and unite his
desires and activities with the functions of

[1] Ethics of Naturalism, p. 135.

the larger organism of which he is a member. Not only is there an actual solidarity between the individual and the whole, but a subjective reflection of the same fact, — sympathy with the feeling of others. The new factors of heredity and evolution thus supply for the first time a scientific foundation for the moral unity of all the members with one another and with society as a whole.

Again, Mr. Spencer's book has well presented the agency (which is not to be disputed) of pleasure and pain, and of the expedient and the inexpedient, in assisting to unfold human intelligence until that intelligence became capable of apprehending the higher ideas of right and duty. Happiness is certainly an object of general desire, and is a usual incident of virtuous life; and it is ever attained much more readily and surely, as Mr. Spencer points out, when we do not consciously make it our aim than when we do. Mr. Spencer has shown good sense in avoiding that pit into which most utilitarians fall, of estimating actions merely by their results, and he wisely reaches his ethical principles by the higher path of deduction from the conditions of successful life. To estimate directly the useful, or that which will in a given case supply the greatest happiness to the greatest number, is most certainly a calculation too uncertain, and open to too much personal and class bias, to be made the standard of morality. The current axioms of ethics have been approved by the experience of many generations, and the wise man will accept their authority rather than essay to draw his own moral deductions from the little storehouse of his own personal experience. With most vigorous logical force, Mr. Spencer has laid low the pretensions of the vulgar utilitarianism which founds its theories upon direct calculation of pleasures and pains and individual advantage, ignoring the claims of the social organism. Especially has Mr. Spencer done a good service in his effective exposures of Bentham's shortcomings, and in his defence of the idea of *justice* as far

more simple and more clear and more accepta-
ble, as an ethical guide, than that standard of
the happiness of the majority which Bentham
would substitute for it.

In all these points we gladly agree with Mr.
Spencer. The factors in every ethical system
are the same. The difference lies in the relative rank given to each. The fatal defect of
the new ethics is that it would elevate the
incidental concomitants to the supreme place,
while the higher essential features it would
degrade to subordinate *rôles*. Though Mr.
Spencer's desire to harmonize the Intuitive
and Utilitarian Schools has saved him from
sinning as badly in these respects as some
others who have essayed to expound to us the
moral teachings of modern science, nevertheless
he has not avoided, it seems to me, many
noticeable and momentous errors. In his use
especially of the principle of evolution, he has
run more than once on the shoals of fallacy.
That the theory which in botany and zoology
had given us such new insight into nature,

should be applied by Mr. Spencer to the domain of morals, was only what was to be expected. In itself, it is not to be regretted. A principle so universal and potent as this, must have some light to throw on the problems of ethics. But like all important principles, it is one that is apt to be over-worked and carried to exaggeration. There springs up soon a false counterpart of it, which seizes on the credentials of its more sober companions and runs riot, imposing on the confidence of careless minds.

So it has been with the principle of development. In its legitimate sphere as the doctrine that describes the unfolding process by which certain determinate germs evolve according to orderly law, a process proceeding, not by accident, but in pre-ordained paths and with defined limits as well as liberties, evolution is a great truth. But the transmutation hypothesis, into which the idea of evolution is too often exaggerated, which recognizes no initial bud as preceding its flower, but only a

formless chaos; no law in the developing
process, but only the selection of fortuitous
chance; and which recognizes no boundaries to
its wild career, — has as different a claim on our
regard as it is radically diverse in character.

Unfortunately, however, this is the form of
speculation which is now most popular, and
Mr. Spencer in his " Data of Ethics " seems to
have been strongly possessed by this madness
of the hour, whose ambition is to erase all
contrasts, and everywhere explain the highest by the lowest.   In his theory of the origin
of our sense of duty he has confounded assistance with production, and occasion with
cause, and in his selection of the ultimate
end of ethics he has failed to see the signifi-
cance of that great law of evolution to whose
study he has devoted such time and labor.
Even Mr. Spencer's own disciples, I think,
must admit that the " Data of Ethics " is, in
many respects, the weakest volume in the
series of his Synthetic Philosophy.

SUCH, in general, is my estimate of the "Data of Ethics." But so severe an arraignment of the work of an acknowledged master deserves, of course, specifications and proofs. Let me state, then, some of the particular points most open to objection.

I. In the first place, I would call attention to the fact that Mr. Spencer, with the purpose of giving us a strictly objective system of ethics, takes as his moral measure the external elements of conduct, — the outward act, and its result on happiness. Man is treated, not as a being possessed of consciousness and will, but as a sentient mechanism that moves by compulsion of certain forces in a necessitated path; and so Mr. Spencer gives up a good deal of his space to the physical and biological views of conduct. The nutrition of polyps, the circulation of blood in mollusks, the wanderings of a fish in search of food, the motions of a carnivorous animal in way-laying its prey, and of bees in building their cells, are discussed as illustrations of evolving morality ; and the characteristics of this ethi-cal progress are said to be "the increased defi-niteness, coherence, and heterogeneity of the motions" as instrumental to the "maintenance of a moving equilibrium." The moral man, in his view, is one whose functions are all dis-charged in degrees duly adjusted to the condi-tions of his existence, and who therefore secures the pleasures connected with such healthful discharge of function. "Actions are completely right only when, besides being conducive to future happiness, special and general, they are immediately pleasurable."

The proper moral motive is "constituted by representations of consequences which the acts naturally produce."[1] The entirely virtu-ous act must be done, not from self-compulsion

[1] Data of Ethics, p. 121.

under a sense of duty or loyalty to the right and the true, but from natural impulse, "with a simple feeling of satisfaction in doing it." [1]

In such expositions there is undoubtedly much ingenuity. But how far outside the proper sphere of morals does much of it lie! How fatally does Mr. Spencer miss those most essential factors in all sound ethical systems, — the motive and the will! In a Hobbes or a Bentham, in the moralists who wrote before the sun of evolution had cast its illuminating rays upon us, it might not perhaps be strange to find them judging of conduct only by its results, without regard to its source. But it seems very strange that a lifelong advocate of evolution, who always wants us to trace the fruit back to the seed, the adult to the embryonic form, before pronouncing upon it, should, in the realm of morals, neglect that from which action springs, and which gives to it its rank, — namely, the motive, — and should fail to see that conduct is only

[1] Data of Ethics, p. 123.

the fruit and manifestation of character. If we ignore the inward aspect of conduct, and consider only its definiteness, coherence, conduciveness to happiness, and other like external features, we might talk not only of the morality of the bee-hive and polyp colony, but of the virtue of a locomotive and the righteousness of a printing-press. There is just as much morality in the latter as in the former. Morality, in fact, does not begin until we rise to the sphere of conscious choice between alternatives recognized as right and wrong, or more or less right.

Every proper moral judgment is a judgment of a *person doing*, not of a *thing* done. Whether an act be pleasure-giving or pain-giving, it has in itself, apart from the agent whence it proceeds, no moral quality.

Whatever ethical quality it has, comes not from its own sweetness or bitterness, immediate or remote results, but from the motive of the actor.

The soldier who, to exhibit his daring,

exposes himself to the enemy's fire, and falls beneath the volley that he has drawn upon himself, we declare guilty of culpable recklessness, if not of suicide. The soldier, whether successful or not, who in an effort to save a wounded comrade falls in a similar way, we honor as a hero. When a daughter administers to her mother by mistake a fatal potion, as happened some time ago in Massachusetts, our deepest pity goes out toward her; but if she had perpetrated the same act with malice prepense, we should have abhorred her as a murderess of the blackest dye.

It is not in the muscular contractions or the nervous currents of our limbs, nor in their outward consequences, that the ethical quality of an act inheres, but in the conscious feeling that was their spring. The railroad president who, in locating a railroad terminus in accordance with his own interests, chooses to render some poor man's heavily mortgaged land marvellously valuable, thus raising him and his family from penury and hardship to wealth,

neither gets nor deserves our moral approbation for such an act. The deed has as little
moral quality as an April shower.

But suppose, on the other hand, the poor
man's daughter, with generous enthusiasm to
relieve her father's embarrassments, but with
unfortunate miscalculation of her strength,
toils with her needle till she renders herself
the prey of consumption, we honor her as a
noble example of filial devotion. Her benevolent spirit, instead of becoming less meritorious
because its purpose does not succeed, is rather
still more exalted because of the pain to self
which it cost.

This determination of the moral qualities of
acts by the conscious purpose in which they
start is one of the fundamental principles of
ethics. A system that ignores it, as does Mr.
Spencer's, must fall inevitably into many errors
and perplexities. It is from this source that
comes his strange statements in the chapter
on Absolute Ethics ; such, for example, as
that "no act producing any pain can be ab-

solutely right." And it is through the same neglect of motives that he places, at the acme of absolute goodness, acts that no one else would credit with any particular virtuousness. Take the heroism of a railway engineer who, seeing a bowlder on the track before him, instead of leaping from his engine to save his own life at the expense of a thousand passengers, stands at his post to the last, and saves a whole train full of people at the cost of rendering himself a cripple for life. The deed is most unselfish in purpose, and most beneficent on the whole in its results; the best possible under the conditions. To make it, nevertheless, partially wrong, as Mr. Spencer declares that all acts involving any pain are, because there was suffering to the self-sacrificing hero connected with it, is to make the difference between right and wrong a matter not determinable by our will, but by our physical or social surroundings; it is to make virtue the shuttlecock of fortune; it is to deny the highest moral worth to all those heroisms which the tragedies of life evoke, as humanity rises on the billows of adversity or fierce temptation which seek to overthrow it; and it is to confer the warmest commendation of the moralist upon those doubly profitable operations of which the eddies of social interaction enable a shrewd eye in balmy hours to avail itself.

The consequences of an act, of course, supply to the conscience the data by which it is enabled to decide whether its virtuous purpose may rightly be externalized in such a deed or not. They supply the *occasion* for a right act, but do not determine the moral quality of the act.

The consequences of an act, in turn, are conditioned upon the external environment. This alters the *form* of the right act; it changes the manner in which a virtuous motive objectifies itself, just as the terra-cotta, plaster, marble, granite, or perhaps snow only, which may be the varying materials in which an artist had to work, would alter the form and appearance of the ideal he intended to embody.

But none of these varied conditions, in which a moral agent works, change the moral quality of his work ; that lies always in the inner sanctuary of the heart, out of which are the issues of the moral life.

" Ideal conduct, such as ethical theory is concerned with," Mr. Spencer tells us, " is not possible for the ideal man in the midst of men otherwise constituted. An absolutely just or perfectly sympathetic person could not live or act according to his nature in a tribe of cannibals," [1] etc.

On the contrary, I say it is just such incongruities between the inner and outer world of a virtuous man that call forth the noblest in him, and display it in the most conspicuous light.

It has been precisely among the degraded and the barbarian, yes, even the treacherous and the cannibal savage, that the missionaries

[1] Data of Ethics, p. 280.

of the gospel, from the time of Ulfilas and
Boniface to that of Livingstone and Patteson
and the noble missionaries who converted the
Fijians from cannibalism to Christianity, have
exhibited the most striking examples of Christian justice and sympathy.

Inauspicious conditions do not prevent or
quench the virtue of a genuine saint, but
make it glow all the more luminously and
purely. They may alter its methods of manifestation, turning it from the paths of peaceful
and friendly service into those of patriotic
defence of the right, or patient submission to
wrong, courageous utterance of the truth to the
very face of the transgressor, or tender forgive-
ness of personal injuries; but whatever varied
form the holy spirit finds it wise and just to
take, does not change its righteousness into
partial wrongness, as Mr. Spencer would have
us think, but it always holds itself on its own
elevated level of entire consecration to the
service of God and man.

This unfaltering fidelity to duty may perhaps cost a man his life, — a consequence which Mr. Spencer regards as an all-sufficient reason for compromising his principles and declaring perfect rectitude in such cases "impossible." But where true moral heroism exists, death is not its defeat, but, as it has well been said, " its canonization, — the assurance of the triumph of the principle, whatever becomes of its servants." The moral law does not need descendants of the righteous man's own blood to transmit his righteousness.

According to Mr. Spencer, ethics, instead of having any immutable character, has various forms according to circumstances. As absolute right-doing is as yet impossible, because society is not yet sufficiently developed, relative right consists in the harmonization of the organism and its impulses to the requirements of the social environment. As this equilibrium always fluctuates with external conditions, physical and social, right and wrong must vary in a similar way.

In "Social Statics," Mr. Spencer told us

that "man needed one moral constitution to
fit him for his original state ; he needed another
to fit him for his present state."   And in a similar strain in the "Data of Ethics," Mr. Spencer
speaks of "changing systems of ethics proper
to changing ratios between warlike activities
and peaceful activities."   In the evolution of
conduct there is a pre-social stage, and a stage
of tribal antagonism in which war is the normal rule, and an industrial stage in which co-
operation and peace at last become the dictate
of duty.   For one stage of social development
there is a moral code of enmity, and for another
a moral code of amity, and for each varying
mixture or point of transition between this
lower and upper plane, an appropriate compromise between these antagonistic moral codes.
"Unlike sets of conclusions respecting human
conduct emerge, according as we are concerned
with a state of habitual or occasional war, or
are concerned with a state of permanent and
general peace." [1]

[1] Data of Ethics, chap. viii.

It has been hitherto one of the chief boasts of morality that while the principles of so many other kinds of knowledge were fluctuating, right was right in all climes and ages. Though rogues and hypocrites and men of the world claimed that it was always permissible to feather their own nests, or at least do as others did, ethics has always presented the rule of duty, the principle of rectitude, as not made of wax, but ever *rectum ;* that is, straight and unbending. But the new ethics will change all that. They will comfort the man who desires to make peace with his conscience, without much self-denial, with the assurance that there is no *absolute* right yet possible, because society is still far from the limit of evolution. Our moral code is and must be a shifting, indefinable " compromise." Its compass pointed in primitive days in a quite opposite direction from that in which it now does ; and in the process of transition, it has been continually veering. Increase of population has abolished the military code of enmity, and forced upon

us the industrial code of amity. Why may
not more increase of population again reverse
the moral code, establishing, for example, hate
instead of love once more as the normal conduct, rendering infanticide a chief duty, and
so on? If such a purely physical circumstance
as the ratio between population and area is to
be held sufficient to shift and even reverse
human morality, duty becomes the mere sport
of accident, — a chameleon changing its colors
with the physical and sociological aspect of
the earth. Such a view of morality strips it
of its authority. It makes man, in his highest
attributes, the creature of circumstance, and
contradicts that belief in our freedom and
responsibility that is essential to our moral life.
Wherever the moral vision has once gained
clear sight of the fundamental principles of
morality, it knows that they can never change.
That malice should ever be right and benevolent feelings wrong, that desire for injustice instead of justice should ever have had or may
have a place in any sound moral code, is incon-

ceivable. Circumstances, of course, have been and often may be inharmonious to the moral intuitions ; but our duty is not to adjust our moral sentiments to fit the circumstances, and by some "mush of moral compromise" attain a comfortable equilibrium, but it is rather, by resolute exertion of our will, to control and subjugate the conditions till they give the moral law its lawful place. Of course, such an effort may fail. He who strives to maintain the pure moral law in an inharmonious environment will probably suffer much, may lose his life before he succeeds. But does it follow, as Spencer would have us think, that a lower and compromised system of ethics, on the scale of the opposing forces, ought in such conditions to be at once substituted ?

In the scales of the new ethics loss of life may be naturally reckoned the sure condemnation of any course of conduct, and even the suffering of a little pain remove an act from the sphere of the absolutely right. But wherever the moral nature retains its ancient nobility, there it is recognized that worldly failure, and even death, are not the worst of things, and that righteousness is worth all that the most inharmonious and uncomfortable environment may exact of it. And in the providence of the Divine Ordainer of the moral law it is just these innocent sufferings of the faithful few, who at such bitter cost refuse to bow the knee to the lower morality of their social environment, that open the eyes of men about them to discern, one after another, the stars of eternal truth.

The theorist who endeavors to put the essence of the moral quality where it does not belong, will naturally involve himself in difficulties, and think morality the creature of circumstances, and pure righteousness only feasible in a perfectly evolved society; but it is only necessary to transfer the seat of the ethical quality from the external act, where it has been so erroneously placed, to the inner realm of purpose and will, to which alone it belongs, to solve all these puzzles.

The immutability of morality lies not in any fixed physical acts, but in the unchanging principles, — to do that which the conscience declares right, to maintain the just and benevolent spirit.

By what acts this just and loving spirit may manifest itself must be learned by experience. These acts will vary in different social circumstances. The evolutionists have presented with great force these variations of current morality in different nations and ages. They have laid great stress upon the diverse judgments pronounced on the same acts by different peoples, as facts upsetting the whole intuitive system of ethics. But it is only necessary to remember that it is not in the external act, but in the motive, that the moral quality lies; that it is not for the special judgments as to practical means and methods, but only for the few self-evident principles of just and loving purpose, that any infallibility is claimed, to see how far aside from the mark these critical arrows fall.

CHAPTER IV.

IN the next place, I take issue upon the statement that the ultimate moral aim is happiness. Here, it seems to me, is a fundamental error that vitiates Mr. Spencer's whole system of morals. He opens the "Data of Ethics" with a survey of conduct and its course. Moral conduct is a part of conduct at large. As we ascend the scale of creation we find the adjustments of ends to means better and more numerous. There is a greater elaboration of life; it is prolonged in time; it becomes broader, embracing more varied activities. Thus the quantity of life is increased. The evolution of conduct is measured by that adjustment of means to ends by which the aggregate of the actions of the developed being is both widened and elongated. But the individual cannot reach his completest life alone. His highest development depends upon that of the race, upon that of society. "Evolution becomes the highest possible when the conduct simultaneously achieves the greatest totality of life in self, in offspring, and in fellow-men." Good conduct is that which conduces to any one of these three forms of life. Good conduct becomes the best "when it fulfils all three classes of ends at the same time."[1]

This is not a bad beginning. It is a logical outcome of the evolution theory. It is a path which, consistently pursued, would have led to the discernment and enunciation of an ultimate end of Nature's ascending path, a consummate fruit of all the cosmic effort which would rightfully present itself as the supreme end of all moral agents; namely, the highest perfection of the highest class of beings that we have to deal with.

And in several other passages Mr. Spencer seems almost to have decided to adopt this

[1] Data of Ethics, p. 26.

logical outcome of his philosophic theory as the supreme end of his system of ethics. He admits as true in a sense "the doctrine according to which perfection or excellence of nature should be the object of pursuit;" for, as he says, "it tacitly recognizes that ideal form of being which the highest life implies and to which evolution tends."[1] He even finds a partial truth in the theological theory of the Divine Will, supernaturally revealed, as the standard of morals. For if we substitute for it its scientific equivalent, "the naturally revealed end toward which the Power manifested through Evolution works, then, since evolution has been and is still working toward the highest life, it follows that conforming to those principles by which the highest life is achieved, is furthering that end."[2]

If, then, Mr. Spencer had taken as his ultimate moral end this highest life of the highest order of beings in existence, — namely,

[1] Data of Ethics, p. 172.   [2] Ibid., p. 171.

the fullest and noblest perfection of the spirit of humanity, — this would have constituted a noble object as the goal of the Ethics of Evolution. Mr. Spencer seemed almost to have advanced to it, having progressed as far as to "totality of life, special and general," as the end toward which the development process moves. He needed only to add the further but most important element, "*elevation* of life," to its length and breadth, as a measure of the evolution of conduct, and he would have given the new ethics a worthy keystone.

But suddenly he stops short and faces in quite another direction, and asks, Why should we promote life? There is no reason for so doing, he says, unless life has a surplus of pleasure, — a surplus which is larger, the greater the totality of life. "Taking into account immediate and remote effects on all persons, the good is universally the pleasurable." [1] "Conduciveness to happiness is

[1] Data of Ethics, p. 30.

the ultimate test of perfection in a man's nature." [1] "Acts are good or bad according as their aggregate effects increase men's happiness or increase their misery." [2] "The absolutely right in conduct can be that only which produces pure pleasure,—pleasure unalloyed with pain anywhere. By implication, conduct which has any concomitant of pain, or any painful consequence, is partially wrong." [3]

Virtue, in Mr. Spencer's system, has no intrinsic worth or authority. Its worth and authority come only from its usefulness as a means subservient to the happiness of the man or his fellows. The paramount worth of righteousness over pleasure has always been a cardinal point of ethics. But Mr. Spencer would put "surplus of pleasure" at the summit of morality, and make of righteousness and duty mere servants that are to procure for mankind the greatest amount

[1] Data of Ethics, p. 34.
[2] Ibid., p. 40. [3] Ibid., p. 261.

of gratification. Mr. Spencer has criticised most severely the methods of Bentham, but he has in fact adopted his ultimate *end*. And much as he makes of righteousness, much as he inculcates the pursuit of truth and perfection, and the practice of love, purity, mercy, they are never in his system the supreme and essential *ends*, but mere *means*, subordinate to the attainment of happiness.

Now, to put at the summit of ethics any such end is to subvert its fundamental order. The distinctions between the right and the expedient, between virtuous and prudent acts, are native to all languages, are essential to any sound system of morality. A noble character, a well-intentioned act, are good things, not simply because they will conduce to happiness; they are good irrespective of whether they bring happiness or not. This is the sure testimony of man's conscience. Honesty is right, not simply because it is the best policy, but because it is the plain dictate of conscience. The reason why a man on the witness-stand is bound to tell the truth about a friend's crime is not that it will give a surplus of pleasure ; on the contrary, it is very easy to suppose instances (every day there are cases occurring) where pleasure, both that of the individual concerned and of the general public, would be much better promoted by the suppression of the truth. Nevertheless, to declare the truth, and not a lie, is right, because it is the requirement of eternal laws that demand this as the only fit relation of word to fact. Nay, more than this, the moral sense, whenever it is fully developed, makes us feel that the very fact that the man practises honesty only out of policy, eliminates from his honesty its quality of virtue.

"Acts are good or bad according as their aggregate effects increase men's happiness or increase their misery," says Mr. Spencer. Let us test this ethical standard by some familiar facts, and see if it is a correct measure of moral worth, or if moral ideas have been

formed under its implicit guidance, as Mr.
Spencer says. In the first place, the seeking
of pleasure for one's self ought to be, in
accordance with his theory, one of the chief
duties of man. We recognize it, indeed, as
quite proper, when not incompatible with
other claims; but no one regards it as a
duty, the neglect of which he feels to be
a sin. It is a *privilege* simply, which he is
at full liberty to enjoy or not. If conduciveness to happiness is the only test of the
moral quality of an act, why is the giving of
a particular gratification to a friend universally reckoned as much more moral than the
giving of that same gratification to one's self;
and why is the taking away of a pleasure
from a friend reckoned a bad action, while
the dropping it from my own sum of happiness, so far from being deemed a bad
action, is reckoned either as a thing morally
indifferent, or, perhaps, as in a case of sacrifice for another's sake, is regarded as of the
very highest order of virtue? The happi-

ness produced or removed is in each case
the same, and the moral quality, according
to Spencer's standard, should be the same ;
but in point of fact, every one recognizes
that there is a radical difference in the moral
quality of the acts, according as they aimed
to benefit one's self or benefit others.

Again, the pursuit of agriculture and manufacture, rather than a hunting life, has been
shown by Mr. Spencer to be most essential
to social advancement and to the increase of
general happiness. "Conduct gains ethical
sanction," he tells us, "as it becomes more
and more industrial." Nevertheless, these
special activities are neither ranked as virtues by the moral sense of mankind, nor is
abstention from them reckoned sin. In the
most civilized and industrial nations, when
war becomes necessary, martial conduct has
quite as much, usually far more, ethical sanction than the ploughing of the fields. The
industrious mechanic who stays at home and
tends his shop ought to be reckoned, accord-

ing to this standard, as of higher virtue than
the patriot who fights for his country's honor.
But, as we all know, this is far from being
the case. Similarly, thrift and avarice, as the
political economists tell us, have done and
still do much more for the welfare of society
than charity or piety. Yet the former certainly rank far below the latter in the moral
scale. The custom of blood revenge — an
eye for an eye, and a tooth for a tooth —
has been in the past, and is still, one of the
most powerful deterrents from crime. Shall
we call it a virtue ?

Again, the chief factor in the development
of civilization, in the formation of society,
and in the adoption of industrial life, is the
increase of population. This multiplies happiness, not only in the ratio of the multipli-
cation of mankind, but in the ratio of the
more complex activities it forces into action
in man. Increase of population is, according
to Mr. Spencer's view, the very creator of
modern morality. Nothing else, then, if his

system of morals be correct, ought to be a higher and plainer duty than the procreation of offspring. Yet has the tribunal of conscience ever pronounced celibacy or childlessness flagrant and moral sins ? They may be called mistakes or misfortunes, but not transgressions. If there have been people who, from purely religious notions, have looked upon failure to rear offspring as a dereliction of duty to departed ancestors, such cases are more than matched by the races and ages in which celibacy has been reckoned the virtuous state, and procreation sinful.

Especially inconsistent with Mr. Spencer's standard of good conduct is that duty of fidelity to truth and loyalty to a man's sincere opinion and the testimony of facts which he has himself · most eloquently preached and nobly illustrated in his own life. This duty of seeking and proclaiming the pure truth, not looking to see what may be the probable consequences of that truth on our happiness, is one that the champions of evolution are

continually urging. When confronted with
the probable effects of the evolutionary view
of the origin of conscience upon the morals of
the rising generation, they repel with indignation the idea that its acceptance should be
made dependent on an estimate of these good
or bad effects, but maintain that it should be
judged only by its inherent truth or falsehood.
And Mr. Spencer and his followers have many
times scored severely those who cater to the
popular prejudices and superstitions of the day
rather than come out boldly on the side of the
new truths which they have seen.

But now, if we adopt Mr. Spencer's standard
of the right, — namely, that which is conducive
to happiness, special and general, — why this
devotion to truth in scorn of consequences ?
Suppose that the present belief in the divine
or intuitive character of conscience be an
illusion ? Nevertheless, it is evident that the
effort to disabuse the world of that belief
will bring great pain to all Christian believers ;
the illusion (if it be one) has done much for

the happiness of mankind, and is still doing
much, consoling the innocent and injured, and
restraining the wicked. What reason (if we
take conduciveness to happiness for our standard of the right) is there for destroying that
illusion? The fact that, in spite of all this,
Mr. Spencer and his followers regard it as both
a right and a duty to dispel it, shows that
practically they do not, and can not, hold by
their own standard of right, but recognize in
the claims of truth a higher end than
happiness.

Or take, as a further illustration, any of
those illusions or misconceptions (there are
plenty of them still in the world) that are so
instrumental in casting over life that shim-
mering halo that chiefly makes existence
tolerable to a large part of the world. The
pleasing fiction comforts the heart in its
distress and supports it in its perplexities.
Why rudely take away the image which is
giving such happiness? Because, it is doubtless answered, the truth will give greater

happiness. But while a Theist rationally believes this, is it a thing that, in the special case where a reform is proposed, has been inductively proved? Not at all. It can hardly be said, even as a general truth, to have been inductively established. Has the progress of knowledge, as a matter of fact, given man more contentment? It has, it is true, saved him from baseless fears ; but it has, on the other hand, removed precious consolations. It has supplied external conveniences ; but it has disturbed the inward waters with distressing doubts and insoluble problems. As Lecky has well said, "The imagination, which is altogether constructive, contributes more to our happiness than the reason, which, in the sphere of speculation, is mainly critical and destructive. The rude charm which in the hour of danger or distress the savage presses so confidently to his breast, the sacred picture which is believed to shed a hallowing and protecting influence over the poor man's cottage, can bestow a more real consolation

in the darkest hour of human suffering than
can be afforded by the grandest theories of
philosophy. The first desire of the heart is to
find something on which to lean. The first
condition of happiness, to common minds, is
the exclusion of doubt. A credulous and
superstitious nature may be degraded, but in
the many cases where superstition does not
assume a persecuting or appalling form, it is
not unhappy; and degradation, apart from
unhappiness, can have no place in utilitarian
ethics. No error can be more grave than to
imagine that when a critical spirit is abroad,
the pleasant beliefs will all remain, and the
painful ones alone will perish. To introduce
into the mind the consciousness of ignorance and the pangs of doubt is to inflict or
endure much suffering which may even survive
the period of transition. 'Why is it?' said
Luther's wife, looking sadly back upon the
sensuous creed which she had left, 'that in our
old faith we prayed so often and so warmly,
and that our prayers are now so few and so
cold?'"

Where, then, ignorance *is* bliss, and to disabuse men's minds of pleasant hallucinations
is considerably to diminish their happiness, as
it is in many cases, what consistent ground is
there in the Spencerian ethics for the rigorous
search after truth and the unfaltering pro-
clamation of whatever fact is found? The
fact, however, that not only mankind in general,
but the evolutionist school in particular, insist
most strongly on this uncalculating pursuit
and unhesitating enunciation of truth as a
supreme virtue, shows that it is more than
a means to happiness, and that there are
other things besides those which conduce to
surplus of pleasure that are right of themselves.

The fact is, that instead of its usefulness for
the production and extension of happiness
being the unfailing test of the rightness of an
action, it is, on the contrary, in not a few cases,
precisely the detachment of an act from all
considerations of pleasure or pain or expediency
that gives it its elevation in the moral scale.
This is the case, for instance, in many acts of

heroism, such as the return of Regulus to his death at Carthage in observance of his promise, or the unswerving obedience to orders by the Six Hundred who made the famous charge at Balaclava.

There is no better test of the correctness of any proposed ethical standard than the application of it to the qualities exhibited in those grand historic acts which by common consent keep their place at the head of the world's roll of honor. In the question just discussed we found the Spencerian standard disclosing its inadequacy. Let us look at another similar point. Not satisfied with putting the virtuousness of any act in its tendency to promote happiness, Mr. Spencer goes on to lay it down (and it is of course a logical deduction) that no act is absolutely good if it produces any pain. It is evident, then, that none of those noblest acts of martyrdom and patriotism, — the self-sacrifice of a Huss or an Arnold von Winkelried, — are any longer entitled to be reckoned among the supremely virtuous deeds. They must give place to such more politic actions as can contrive to combine with their ministry to others' happiness a thrifty security of one's own.

Does the reader desire an example of what Mr. Spencer considers an "absolutely good action," — one that in the ethics of evolution is to be ranked as the climax of rectitude? Here is what, in strict accordance with his theory, he singles out as the *ne plus ultra* of good conduct. [1]

Foremost, the action of a healthy mother suckling a healthy infant; or the relation of a father to a sympathetic and docile son. Next, the life of a poet, painter, or musician who obtains his living by acts that are directly pleasurable to him, while they yield, immediately or remotely, pleasure to others. Then, certain of the so-called benevolent acts, such as combine the obtaining of pleasure for self with the giving it to another; as, for example, when one who has slipped is saved from

[1] Data of Ethics, pp. 261, 262, 263.

a fall by a bystander, or when an explanation removes a misunderstanding between friends.

And on the same principle he might have added to this list of "absolutely good actions" the barterings and exchanges of commerce, free trade and free lunches, professional philanthropy, time-serving, flattery, and social toadyism, bribery, concubinage, and well-regulated prostitution, — all of which likewise combine advantage to one's self with the pleasure of the other party concerned.

That which the moral sense of the world has always estimated as the greatest addition to the moral worth of an action, — namely, its *cost* to one's self, — is reckoned by Mr. Spencer as impairing its absolute rightness. The noble refusal of a Jerome of Prague to recant his faith was very far from absolutely right, for it brought a great deal of suffering upon both himself and the community whose religious torpor it painfully awakened. But the action of the opera-singer who can put a thousand dollars a night into her own pocket while tickling the ears of the people, is conduct absolutely right, because both sides profit by the transaction! This certainly is *not* a scientific analysis of our ethical notions. If it be true, it is a radical overturning of the fundamental principles of morality.

Happiness cannot properly, then, be taken as our ultimate end. But suppose, for the sake of the argument, we grant this and take happiness for our ultimate end, and conduciveness to happiness as our test of the absolutely right: have we then a standard that can be scientifically used to determine the merit of actions?

By no means. For what is the happiness we shall take as our standard? Happiness is not a thing of a single kind, but of many kinds, essentially different in their claims on the regard of an intelligent being. There is happiness of the belly, happiness of the eye and ear, happiness of the mind, happiness of the soul. Which of these shall we take as our end? Which ought all men to aim at, on the Spencerian theory? The aim of life in this system is, remember, to make most sure of surplus of pleasure, special and general. By the religious man, of course, the highest pleasure is to be found in the satisfaction of his spiritual nature. But for the man in whom this part of his nature is little developed, and in whom the understanding predominates, pleasure consists in the gratification of intellectual tastes. The sensual man, in his turn, finds his happiness, as naturally and exclusively, in satisfying the demands of his bodily appetites. Men of each class will place the end of life in the attainment of that kind of happiness which to them is the desirable kind.

Happiness is not an entity or a quality in itself, but a simple equilibrium between desire and attainment. So far from being something primary and absolute, and so fit for being an ultimate end, it is a result, often quite accidental, of varying and transitory causes. It is a part, not a whole, and supposes always the craving or felt lack, the out-reach and struggle for the object of its longing, and the chance of success in this struggle; in fact, all these inner vital needs, desires, and tendencies, and those outer supplies, by which a new equilibrium is reached. The only thing that the idea of happiness fixes is this equilibrium between desire and attainment. But this equilibrium, as all know, can be found as much on the lowest as on the highest level of life. It comes to the ignorant and the brutal not less than to the intelligent and the spiritual-minded.

To make happiness, then, the ultimate aim is to give the man who would know his duty a compass that would change its direction in the hands of every different class in the community, according to the plane of development on which that class stands. The variableness of the notion or standard of virtue amongst different races and ages is one of the standing objections made by the

utilitarian school against the intuitive moralists. But the variability of the idea of happiness is still greater.[1] Not only do the
notions of happiness of a worm-eating Aus-
tralian or a Polynesian cannibal differ *toto
cœlo* from those of the refined European, but
in the same nation and age the conceptions
of beatitude vary almost as much. Even
with the same individual they vary with
each shifting mood. If happiness is to be
of any use as an ethical end, we must fix on
some one kind of happiness as the standard.
What kind does Mr. Spencer select?

When we make this inquiry, we find
another defect of Mr. Spencer's system. He
makes no clear distinctions between different
kinds of happiness as possessing different
worth, but practically lumps them all together, and asks simply for the sum-total.
It is surplus of pleasure, the maximum gratification, special and general, accompanied

[1] Data of Ethics, p. 185.

with the least pain, that is the measure of
good according to Mr. Spencer.[1] A qualified
and average supremacy is allowed, it is true,
to the more compound and representative
feelings over the more simple and presentative; but this is due simply to the experienced benefit of such a course for the
aggregate of happiness.[2] The higher gratifications have no *intrinsic* superiority claimed
for them. Perfection of nature is of worth
only because it is estimated to bring a
greater aggregate of pleasure.

Let us see then to what kind of conduct
such an ethical end might be expected to conduct us. For nine tenths of the human race,
at least, what are the easiest and surest means
of gaining happiness ? What else but those
means that will gratify the desires of the
senses ? The bulk of mankind are swayed
most powerfully by their bodily appetites,
and the happiness which in Mr. Spencer's

[1] Data of Ethics, pp. 40, 43, 268.
[2] Ibid., pp. 112, 113.

system is their being's end and aim can be
most readily attained, often can only be attained, by satisfaction of these appetites. For
obtaining the greatest aggregate of pleasure
in the human race, the chief thing to be
aimed at is healthiness of the bodily organs
and an abundant supply for the animal crav-
ings. Soundness of the liver and plenty of
sweets for the mouth count more for happiness with a majority of the human race
than largeness of the intellect or pureness
of conscience.

Now compare with this the declarations of
the moral sense. It looks at the character
of the different kinds of gratifications, and
distinguishes them as of essentially varying
worth. Satisfaction of the intellect is a more
worthy satisfaction than that of the appetite;
satisfaction of the affections is higher than
that of the senses; and satisfaction of the
moral nature is highest of all. The superiority of our moral nature, on Mr. Spencer's
theory, is due simply to its greater service-

ableness to the sum-total of happiness.
"Quantity of pleasure being equal," Bentham used to say, "push-pin is as good as
poetry;" and Mr. Spencer's reasoning often
seems based on the same implication. But
the instinctive moral sense of the world recognizes a difference of value in our pleasures,
according as it is the lower or the higher
part of our nature that is satisfied. The satisfaction of the higher nature occupies a
superior rank in the moral order, independent of its greater or less aggregate of pleasure. To awaken reason and conscience in a
community is good, though it ruin forever
the animal content in which its members had
dozed, and even though it fill their hearts
with spiritual longings never to be entirely
satisfied. The discontent of an aspiring heart
is a nobler thing than the completest satisfaction of any clam at the highest of high
water. Pascal on his bed of pain, or Savonarola at the stake, is a better sight, morally,
than any thousands of lives that have been

passed merely in eating and sleeping and aimless ease.

The various satisfactions of our nature differ not merely in quantity, but in quality, as John Stuart Mill was forced eventually to grant. To use the admission of this most acute defender that utilitarianism has yet had, "a little of one of the higher pleasures is worth as much as a great quantity of one of the lower."

"It is better to be a dissatisfied man," Mill nobly declared, "than a satisfied pig." It was a sentiment that did honor to the great English philosopher, and in which, I have no doubt, Herbert Spencer would concur. But as soon as it is recognized, it pulls down every mere "*pleasure*" standard of morals; for as the agreeable has no scale of perfection, we can only justify the superior value of one pleasure to any other of equal quantity by admitting that happiness alone is not the criterion of ethics. If a satisfied pig is not better than a dissatisfied man, then we must acknowledge that "surplus of pleasure" does not supply the standard of goodness, but that the moral element has an intrinsic superiority in kind which rightly commands the will. But when it is admitted that the satisfaction of our higher nature is of more importance and obligation than the satisfaction of our lower nature, irrespective of the question on which side lies the greater intensity or aggregate of pleasure, then the cause of hedonism is virtually surrendered; for it is acknowledged that there is another factor superior in its claims to "surplus of pleasure."

But in point of fact, a defender of Mr. Spencer would probably reply, Does not higher development of nature bring with it new avenues of pleasure and more abundant and varied enjoyments and resources for amusements, and thus a greater aggregate of happiness? Does not the very fact that we choose the higher pleasure show that it is really the greater in quantity?

I do not think so. Take an instance, and
examine it. When, for example, I decide to
stay at home to perform a very disagreeable
task which I feel to be a duty to a suffering friend, rather than go to the theatre,
I do not choose this satisfaction of my conscience rather than of my senses because it is
more pleasant on the whole, but because it
has a legitimate supremacy. The impulse to
satisfy the conscience comes, not from recognizing a surplus of pleasure in that direction, but from a recognition of its authority
and lawful command, whether pleasant or
not. The happiness that attends the virtuous choice is not the *cause* of that choice,
but an incidental after-effect. The satisfaction of the mind or the conscience is undoubtedly a nobler satisfaction than that of
intoxication. But in intensity, in complete satisfaction for the time being, the bliss that the
opium-eater obtains by purely physical means
exceeds that given by the intellectual acquisition or by any virtuous act. If a chemist

should some day find a drug that will be
able to prolong such ecstatic intoxication
indefinitely, without subsequent painful effects, he might carry the whole world, with
one magic sleeping-dose, to the ultimate goal
of the Spencerian morality.

IN the next place, I would ask whether in taking happiness as the ultimate end of conduct, Mr. Spencer is not putting his system of ethics in conflict with his scientific system. The supreme principle of his science and philosophy is that of evolution; and evolution finds its expression in the preservation and unfolding of the individual and of the race. Now, it is assumed that this development of life tends at each step to the production of increased happiness, and that the laws of the development of life give practical moral principles, by following out which, the greatest happiness may be obtained.

Now, in point of fact, is there such a correspondence and concomitance between the steps of evolution and the increase of happiness? On the contrary, in the name of evo-

lution itself, I object to the ultimate end
that Mr. Spencer has presented for human
conduct. The end which should be the
object of our noblest strivings, the worthy
reward for faithful obedience, ought to be
among those ends toward which the whole
Kosmos is plainly toiling, as it mounts, step
by step, the grand stairway of creation. As
we track the course of development through
the geologic ages and the successive ranks of
the animal and vegetable worlds, we plainly
see sensibility, perception, intelligence, will,
and the moral sense constantly increasing.
This steady elevation of life is unmistakable,
no matter how many lives, how many tor-
tures, it costs, provided that .some better
organism, some new faculty, some fuller unfolding of our psychical life may be purchased by the struggle. But for happiness,
evolution seems to have concerned itself only
in a minor degree. The pleasure and pain
of individuals, the destruction of whole
species, do not matter much to Nature when

engaged in some great upward movement.
Hardly do her chariot-wheels make a single
revolution without crushing multitudes.
Hardly can her most consummate product
— the man of superlative genius — tell
whether, in the matter of surplus of pleasure, he has much advantage, if any, over the
turtle that basks for two or three hundred
years on its tropic beach.

There is evidently a grave discrepancy here
between the principle of evolution and the end
and ideal of universal conduct upon which Mr.
Spencer has based his system of ethics; and
the more carefully this is examined, the wider
appears the gap. Evolution, as Mr. Spencer
has presented it, is a law of all living beings,
from the most rudimentary and simple beings
to the highest and most complex. There is
a progressive elevation among these different
orders, and Mr. Spencer essays to show that
conduct evolves *pari passu* as we follow up
the developmental order; and to conform his
moral system to his scientific system it should

do so. But by taking pleasure as the ultimate end and measure of his ethics, this
simultaneous development of the two becomes
impossible; for in the great realm of vege-
tation, and probably in the numerous classes
of the lower animals that possess no speci-
alized nervous system, evolution progresses
from lower to higher stages, without any
corresponding increase in pleasurable sensation.
Though clever theorists have boldly supposed
plants to possess consciousness, there is little
or nothing to prove that they have feelings.
But evolution does not wait for the capacity
of pleasure or pain before beginning to work,
nor is that feeling necessarily attached to
the progressive steps of evolution. *A for-
tiori*, the feeling of pleasure cannot be its
necessary end. When we ascend to a certain
height in the scale of evolution, we find the
sensation of pleasure appearing, and in a
rough way, throughout the upper half of
the scale of animal life, happiness increases in
approximate ratio with the evolution of the

faculties and capacities of animals.   But the
two do not keep step together.   The one
series here runs ahead of the other, there
falls behind its comrade.   In their evolutional
rank, *e. g.*, the snarling hyena and the lean and
hungry wolf stand far above the fat porpoise
and the gentle kangaroo.   But there is little
doubt that in mere happiness these lower
forms have the advantage.   The full-grown cat
is undoubtedly more completely evolved than
the young kitten.   But the playful kitten no
doubt has much more pleasure.   So when we
go up still higher, to the human domain, there
is great room for doubt whether the man is
happier than the chattering monkey or the
contented cow rolling its cud under its tongue
all day long.   There is a great probability
that the savage of Tahiti or Samoa, lying under
his bread-fruit tree, gets a greater and more
unalloyed enjoyment from his life than the
civilized European; and it is quite certain
that our frolicsome children get far more
pleasure from their budding and half-developed

natures than we do from the full-bloom of adult and civilized life.

It is a very plausible theory that pleasure follows increase of life, or is the sense of heightened vitality, while pain corresponds to a loss of vitality. But although there are many facts that agree with this theory, there are a multitude of other facts that do not agree with it. On the contrary, intense pleasure seems sometimes as deleterious to life as excessive pain; the effort after a fuller life does not bring pleasure, but the reverse. Generally speaking, as Mr. Spencer himself notices in his "Psychology," [1] " Pleasures are the concomitants of *medium activities* where the activities are of kinds liable to be in excess or defect." Again, as an activity becomes more completely organized and passes from its earlier voluntary stage to its completer involuntary stage, we find that in this further stage, where it has become a settled habit, the pleasure or the pain, whichever it was, that

[1] Vol. i. Section 123, p. 277.

was earlier experienced, fades away, as it passes gradually out of the sphere of attention into the realm of unconsciousness.

It is claimed by the laudators of our modern industrial progress that the increase in the amount of wealth produced affords a vastly greater means of comfort. "But it is doubtful," as Mr. Sorley has observed,[1] "whether this increase has always been sufficient to keep up with the growth of population; and it is certain that every society whose territory is limited must, when its numbers have increased beyond a certain point, begin to experience the diminishing returns which Nature yields for the labor expended upon it. Indeed, the tendency to an excess in the rate of increase of population over that of means of subsistence is one of the chief causes which make it so difficult to assert that civilization leads to greater happiness. But even although the average quantity of wealth be greater now than before, it must be remembered that social

[1] Ethics of Naturalism, p. 181.

wealth is measured by its total amount, whereas happiness depends on the equality with which that amount is distributed. Yet the present industrial *régime* tends to the accumulation of immense wealth in a few hands rather than to its proportionate increase throughout the community. The industrial progress which increases the wealth of the rich has little to recommend it if it leaves the laboring poor at a starvation wage.

Moreover, the very nature of economic production seems to imply an opposition between social progress and individual well-being. For the former, in demanding the greatest possible amount of produce requires an excessive and increasing specialization of labor. Each worker must perform that operation only to which he has been specially trained or which he can do best. And in this way "industrialism tends to occupy the greater part of the waking hours of an increasing proportion of human lives, in the repetition of a short series of mechanical movements which call out a bare minimum of the faculties of the worker, dwarf his nature, and reduce his life to a mere succession of the same monotonous sensations." In spite, therefore, of immense improvements of the general conditions of well-being, it is still difficult to say that the happiness of the average human life has been much increased by the march of industrial progress.

Nay, take the case of the favored children of modern civilization, and is there not more or less of the same doubt whether their higher evolution is attended with a corresponding increase of happiness.

Happiness, as we have seen, consists in the perfect equilibrium of our felt needs and desires with the possibility of satisfying them. But it is a well-observed law of life that with the increase of powers and sensibilities that give added gratifications, the desire for such gratifications increases with even greater rapidity. The needs of the infant or of the savage are very few; they are mostly those of the animal order, and are very easily satisfied. A full stomach, a place to lounge in the sun, a few playthings, bring complete content. But with the adult and the civilized man the desires of life are enormously increased. A hundred luxuries undreamed of by the savage, a thousand longings and passions unawakened in the child, now demand satisfaction as daily necessities; rich clothing, furniture, multitudinous inventions and conveniences must be ours, or we are miserable. Social ambition and jealousies, patriotic and family pride, intellectual and religious aspirations, desire for fame, soul sympathy, eternal truth, — a countless throng of insatiable wants possess the modern man. And though the sum of his powers and gratifications has also been immensely increased, it does not begin, in most cases, to balance the sum-total of the things of which he feels the lack.

Again, it is a peculiar but undoubted law of human psychology that the intensity of the sensation of any evil or disappointment is

more intense than the sensation of any good
or attained pleasure. Two days of hunger and
starving make far deeper impression on the
memory than a dozen days of feasting; and
the pain that comes from a loss of a thousand
dollars a year, with its necessitated retrench-
ment, far exceeds the pleasure we receive from
an equivalent addition to our yearly income.
No completest satisfaction of high desire gives
the adult such intoxication of happiness as a
drum or a bon-bon will give to the little child.
In proportion as human life is evolved to
higher stages and the nervous sensibility becomes more susceptible, suffering becomes more
intense, and desire and longing stretch over
longer periods. The moments of satisfaction
are relatively less. The taste grows more and
more critical, aspirations become more exact-
ing; the gap between our wishes and our power,
between our duties and our tastes, between our
theories and our beliefs, between our infinite
passions and our finite capabilities, daily grows
broader; and happiness becomes a more dis-

tant and inconstant goddess, more rarely coming forth as our wooing becomes more and
more frantic.

And it is well to notice also that it is not
those who have pursued pleasure, or taken
good care to secure it, who have especially
carried forward the evolution of the human
race. If the progressive evolution of being
had waited upon happiness for its advancement, had refused to step forward except upon
the stepping-stones of pleasure, it might have
waited forever. On the contrary, we all know
at what a cost of painful effort the progress
of civilization, the intellectual and spiritual
development of our race, has been purchased.
Even in the realm of animal life, every new
variation which marks a higher stage of ad-
vancing evolution had its beginning in a rup-
ture of the simpler harmony that previously
existed. And so in human society, there can
be no progress and better adjustment of life
to its surroundings without involving at the
start some more or less painful disturbance

of the old social equilibrium and happiness.
The use of the hands as forefeet had to be
surrendered, as Darwin observes, before they
could become serviceable to hurl stones and
wield weapons. So in the development from
the hunter's life to the shepherd's, from the
life of savage freedom to that of tribal restric-
tions, the transition at first must have greatly
disturbed the former comfortable relations.
" The highest intelligences," well says Émile
Beaussire,[1] " are those which contain themselves with most difficulty, which foresee most
fully all the causes of uncertainty and error.
And these noble intelligences are most often
united to the most delicate and irritable sensibility, the most accessible to discouragements,
to anger against all the obstacles which from
without and within keep them back from the
truth. Nothing of that which honors humanity in the intellectual order would have
been accomplished if there had not been men
whose thought elevated itself above the ex-

[1] Les Principes de la Morale, p. 205.

clusive preoccupation with their happiness.
And neither would anything of that which
honors humanity in the moral order have been
accomplished under such conditions. Would
that which sees no higher than to preserve
the *mens sana in corpore sano* have ever been
capable of devotion? Would it ever have been
capable of heroism? Mr. Spencer sees only
a last vestige of the most ancient superstitions
in the glorification of grief, dear still to certain Stoic and Christian souls. It was, he
holds, the idea of the jealousy of the gods at
human happiness that made primitive men
satisfy them by offering to them the spectacle
of most atrocious sufferings. Our modern virtue and piety, he charges, preserve the trace
of these gross beliefs when they find merit in
nobly enduring suffering. I know not how
legitimate is this deduction. But there is
something else in the idea of nobleness which
attaches itself to suffering courageously supported or even audaciously braved. Not only
is the suffering a test for virtue, as has always

been recognized, but the field for suffering seems to enlarge with the progress of virtue. Whoever names patriotism names a capacity for suffering greater than all the evils of our native land. Whoever names charity names a capacity for suffering grander than all the evils of humanity. What sufferings spring from the family virtues! 'Happy they who have no children' has well been said of parents. We miss a virtue whenever we lose an occasion for suffering."

An English poetess, who had herself been a severe sufferer, pathetically asks, —

" Is it so, O Christ in heaven, that the highest suffer
        most ?
   That the mark of rank in nature is capacity of pain,
   And the anguish of the singer makes the sweetness of
        the strain ? " [1]

Certainly it often seems to be so. The increase of knowledge is verily an increase of sorrow, a root of discontent and perplexity. The evolution from instinct to consciousness

[1] From Twilight Hours, by Sarah Williams. London : Strahan, 1868.

and from consciousness to self-consciousness is ever attended by the development of care and anxiety; and as life enlarges and deepens into a true spiritual existence, it finds the higher powers and yearnings and responsibilities, to a consciousness of which it awakens, more and more out of harmony with its material environment and the selfish social atmosphere in which it is immersed.

Wonderfully as the victories of human intellect have increased man's power, his mastery over nature, and his domestic conveniences, and notably as they have surrounded him with elegancies, luxuries, and beauties that amaze the savage, the man who walks at the summit of our modern civilization is yet probably farther below his ideals, and farther from a perfect equilibrium between his longings and his attainments, than the negro of the Gold Coast. The growth of human ambition and wishes far outstrips the speed of human progress. The life whose delicacy of feeling, clearness of insight, and delicate conscientiousness mark it as standing on the highest plane of evolution, is little likely to be one supremely happy. Rather is it likely to be one profoundly dissatisfied with itself. Discontent with even the most brilliant victories, and aspiration for something grander than all it has ever attained, is the universal mark of the noblest natures.

The deep thought upon insoluble problems, the wide sympathies with all the unavoidable misery of the world, which come with all the finer evolution of character, bring with it as much pain as pleasure, often more pain than pleasure. For pure happiness we look not among the mature and fully developed, so much as among the careless children at their play, or the tropic barbarian lounging in the shade, sucking his banana or sugar-cane in bovine contentment. Mr. Spencer himself, in his work on Sociology, has noticed how preeminently full of fun and merriment and good spirits are the African negroes and the savages of Polynesia.

Now, if happiness be the ultimate end and proper moral aim of man, the Pessimists can make a very strong plea for their thesis that our world is a world constantly growing worse, and that evolution is a colossal blunder in that Unknowable Power that so constantly presses us onward. It is only when both pleasure and pain are recognized, not as ends in themselves, but as means to lift up the soul to a higher spiritual level, and to develop and balance its faculties in a harmonious perfection, that evolution becomes a process which has not its drawbacks.

I do not, of course, mean to deny that pleasure accompanies the process of development. What I maintain is simply that it is a very irregular accompaniment of the evolution of life, an accompaniment so generally alloyed with attending pains and dissatisfactions — noble, perhaps, but none the less real — that the gain of a corresponding surplus of pleasure is doubtful. Increase of pleasure is no more a constant and essential accompaniment of evolution than pain is. The correspondence and concomitance between the progress of evolution and the increase of the surplus of plea-

sure which Mr. Spencer's theory demands is
not found. Where pleasure attends evolution,
it attends it, not as a direct result, but as a
consequent of the other goods, — health, physical force, increased nerve-sensibility, development of the will and the intelligence, especially
the harmony of faculties, which mark the attainment of a higher stage of existence.

But for an evolutionist consistently to make
happiness the ultimate end of his ethical system, he ought to be able to show that it is
more than a *usual incident* of evolution. It
should be shown to be an *essential* element,
regularly progressing with equal steps. The
ultimate end of evolutionary ethics ought to
be something that evolution itself, without a
doubt, aims at and secures, — something that
is *inseparable from the very idea of evolution.*
Now, happiness, as we see, can never maintain a claim to such a place, and Mr. Spencer's
ethical end is therefore inconsistent with the
principles of evolution.

CHAPTER VI.

THE older hedonists not only made pleasure the ultimate end of existence, but
the immediate aim and guide of man. This
was a view which was open to such grave
objection that Mr. Spencer himself has been
one of the warmest in criticising Bentham and
his school for taking such a position. He has
acknowledged and strongly re-stated the ancient truth, — that he who would have happiness must not aim directly for it. While men
fiercely and selfishly struggle for it, it dissolves
within their very grasp; but when they turn
away from the constant anxiety about it to
discharge their duties to others, then of its
own accord it returns, and drops gently and
refreshingly upon them, like morning dew.
Moreover, Mr. Spencer has recognized the im-
possibility of any such comparative measure-
ments of all the various kinds and intensities

of happiness as hedonism, either egoistic or universalistic, requires. Under neither its personal nor its general form, he argues, can the components of happiness be assessed and calculated, so as to form a practicable and trustworthy guide.

Mr. Spencer, therefore, separates here from the utilitarian schools, and makes this one of the cardinal features of his system; namely, that for our immediate aim or guide we must take, not calculation of happiness, but those general rules of conduct which experience has shown to be the best means of giving happiness, special and general. Happiness is a result of laws and conditions, a product of organism and environment. The happiness of any individual is inextricably bound up with the welfare of his fellows, the good order of society, the prevalence of justice, truth, and altruistic habits in the community at large. The best way to secure happiness, then, is to conform to those principles which in the nature of things causally determine happiness. What the moralist must aim at is "the *fundamental conditions* to the achievement of happiness, both special and general." But if the hedonistic calculation of the more immediate means of happiness be impracticable, one would suppose that this calculation of the more remote and general means would be at least equally so. To what shall the common man who wants to know his duty look as a standard ? Mr. Spencer takes refuge in the assumption that the intuitive principles of ethics are laws of general welfare which the experience of the ages has led past intelligence to discover and proclaim. These are to be taken by us as provisionally correct statements of the conditions of human welfare till "illuminated and made more precise by an analytic intelligence."

Here is, indeed, a wide divergence from the older utilitarianism. The evolutionists look upon it as a notable contribution to the science of ethics. I see in it, indeed, a bold and novel move to cover one of the chief

weaknesses of the hedonistic line, but a
move that will not succeed. For in confes-
sing the injuriousness of using happiness, not
only individual, but corporate happiness, as a
proximate end of conduct,[1] Mr. Spencer does
in fact admit its insufficiency as an ultimate
end. How can it deserve to be the last and
highest standard, if not fit at all to be
directly pursued? It may not always be
practicable to apply that which is the true
supreme test, — the absolute good; but in
simple cases it must be not only practicable
to apply it, but it must be the only proper
test: and wherever it is feasible to apply it,
there it must be useful and entirely fitting so
to do. It is not credible that a primary
principle, which is (as Mr. Spencer says of
happiness) the ultimate end to which all
action should be *conducive,* and the real origin of our ideas of virtue and vice, should
nevertheless be (as he afterwards has to
admit) "of little service unless supplemented

[1] Data of Ethics, p. 238.

by the guidance of secondary principles," and that "throughout a large part of conduct, guidance by such comparisons " (*i. e.*, pleasures and pains) should have to be "entirely set aside and replaced by other guidance."[1]

That which is the supreme end of conduct is that which evidently ought to be aimed at by wise and good men. How comes it, then, if happiness be that end, that the pursuit of it is an obstacle to its own attainment? as Mr. Spencer admits is the case. If happiness be our proper end, the *summum bonum* of existence, it is extraordinary that the whole system of Nature ' should have been so arranged as to deny it to him who seeks it most earnestly and directly, and to confer it, instead, upon him who does not care for or labor after it. Such an incongruity would be an incomprehensible anomaly in a system which every where else connects reward with labor, and attainment with effort.

[1] Data of Ethics, p. 156.

Mr. Spencer's theory presents the system of Nature as so irrational that it repels and hinders what it commands. What is the truth? Is it not simply the correct image of the facts of the world? The line of truth is then the line of facts. He who adopts and acts out the truth, falls in line with the universal current. In science wherever we find out a truth and follow it, we find ourselves helped forward by it. But Mr. Spencer says that in morals (if his theory is true) this universal law no longer holds good, but that when one follows the truth and pursues the happiness which is the real end of life, then Nature resists, instead of co-operating with him. Which is more likely, — that Nature is thus contradictory and irrational, or that Mr. Spencer has merely made a mistake in comprehending the ultimate object of life? There is no explanation except the very simple one that the proper end of life is something higher than happiness.

MR. SPENCER'S criticism of Bentham's inductive method of determining right and wrong by direct valuation of the pleasures and pains of a given act is very forcible. But is his own deductive method any less objectionable? When there are some self-evident truths to start from, or first principles possessing intrinsic authority, the deductive method is a good one. But are Mr. Spencer's starting-points of this character? Not at all. They are merely the organic expressions of the past experience of the race. Are these moral discoveries of past generations, then, to be taken as authoritative in themselves, without modern reason needing to verify them, or in spite of what modern reason finds? May the modern man who would know his duty, and who, in obedience to Mr. Spencer's demon-

stration, acknowledges that he is not able
directly to value the aggregate pains and
pleasures of any given act, reasonably take
refuge in the hypothesis that the earlier
ages of humanity were quite equal to such
tasks?

That would be a very fitting position to
be taken by a champion of the Eden story
and the primitive divine illumination of our
race; but it is utterly incompatible with
such views of man's primitive ignorance,
superstition, and degradation, and the great
forward strides of humanity in the last three
centuries, as Mr. Spencer has presented to
us in his works on Sociology.

Before the consistent evolutionist, then,
can accept as fundamental principles these
first laws of morality, handed down by past
experience, so as to use them as fixed
points from which to let down the links of
his deductive logic, he must verify them.
And how can they be verified, except by
the same direct estimation of the pleasures

and pains, special and general, proximate and remote, caused by given acts? To establish scientifically the first principles of ethics, which may constitute the starting-point of his deductive system, Mr. Spencer must use the very method he censures so strongly in Bentham.

The fact is, that unless he adopts the intuitive method, there is no other alternative. Practically, we find that while Mr. Spencer claims to give ethics a new and better basis than that afforded by either the Inductive or the Intuitional school, he shifts from one to the other. In one place, ethical laws which our moral intuitions lay down for us are corrected because they do not conform to his estimate of surplus of pleasure. In another place he tells us that in order to establish the standards from which to deduce practical rules of right, we must ascertain the ideal ethical truths, and form in our minds a model of a perfect man, and consider how he would act in a perfect society. But how this ideally

8

perfect man is to be constructed without the
aid of that moral intuition which Mr. Spencer
would dispense with, we fail to see.

While most unfortunately immovable in his
view of the ultimate moral end, sticking firmly
to his pet "surplus of pleasure," he is as
unfortunately shifting and inconsistent in his
declarations concerning the methods of determining ethical first principles. When
seeking to rout the hedonistic school, he
inveighs against the direct estimation of the
aggregate of happiness. When aiming to demonstrate the superiority of his system over the
Intuitive, he wishes us to have first principles
which are not mere assumptions, but which
express the experience of past ages. When
reviewing another of those current ethical
systems, all whose scalps he would take to
adorn his war-belt, he expresses his surprise
"that a notion so abstract as that of perfection,
or a certain ideal completeness of nature,
should ever have been thought to be one from
which a system of guidance can be evolved."

Yet when he retires from the foray to build up his own system, he turns his back on the very positions that he had previously taken, and would give us, as first principles of absolute ethics, from which all relative ethics are to be deduced, the ideal acts of an ideally perfect man in that fully evolved society which the far-distant future is expected some-time to present.

If utilitarianism, both egoistic and universal, is to be condemned, as Mr. Spencer urges, on the ground of the impracticability of definitely estimating the quantities of pleasure and pain to be weighed against each other, much more difficult of calculation, it seems to me, will it be to determine the character of this ideal man who has reached the summit of human evolu-tion, and to settle the manner in which he will act in a perfectly evolved society, and the amount of variation from this standard that is lawful for the imperfect man in his imperfect surroundings. When Mr. Spencer begins to think what a task he has set the seeker after righteousness, he dare not himself assert its feasibility. Here are his own words : "That it will ever be practicable to lay down precise rules for private conduct in conformity with such requirements, may be doubted."[1] Especially, in that extensive and important field of duty comprehended in beneficence, negative and positive, he finds that his system "has little application, and is not of much assistance." For one who has spent so much time and space in proving the impracticability of the hedonistic calculation, and made that impracticability his chief arsenal of attack on Bentham, and a cogent reason for rejecting the older utilitarian system, this is surely a most humiliating, most fatal confession.

[1] Data of Ethics, p. 283.

ESPECIALLY distinctive of Mr. Spencer's system of ethics is his treatment of our moral ideas and moral sentiments.

Conscience, in the generally accepted view, has been held to be a native, underived faculty. The moral elements have been regarded as innate, simple, necessary, of absolute obligation, universal and immutable. But as modern chemists have decomposed the ancient simple elements, earth, air, fire, and water into their components, so modern psychologists have endeavored to demonstrate that the moral elements are really compound, and they essay to exhibit the lower and coarser factors from which they have been formed by various kinds of cerebral fusion.

By constant mental association of certain elementary sensations, these simpler and lower

feelings grow into a single complex sentiment.
Means are thus inextricably connected with
ends; and soon, as in the case of avarice, the
means, like a French mayor of the palace,
make themselves sovereign, and become objects
of honor and desire on their own account.
The individual learns by experience that his
own interests are inseparably bound up with
those of his fellows, and that the conditions of
prosperous life are everywhere the same; and
thus the immutable, universal conditions of
prosperous life take the place of personal
happiness as the proximate ends of human
pursuit, and soon acquire a sacred character.

These views of the derivative origin of
conscience and its peculiar phenomena had
been urged for many years by the moralists
of the Association school. But the hypothesis, although presented and advocated
with extreme ingenuity by Bentham, James
Mill, John Stuart Mill, and Sidgwick, was seen
to have some decidedly weak points. Individual experience did not give sufficient time

for these moral metamorphoses. The appearance of moral intuitions in as strong, or even stronger, form in youth than in age was an unexplained difficulty. Some further hypothesis was necessary if the derivative character of moral ideas was to be established. It is the distinction of Mr. Spencer, we are assured, that he has supplied this further analysis of psychological chemistry, and solved the crucial problem of ethics.

By introducing the element of hereditary accumulation and transmission it is claimed that he has harmonized the old antagonisms of the Intuitive and Association schools in a theory that embraces the truth contained in both. Moral truths are innate in the present generation. But they are so only because, by a law of inheritance, the experiences of our ancestors have been organized in our brains. The social environment, by its constant pressure upon humanity for ages, has moulded the individual, little by little, into harmony with his social conditions of happiness, till at last they have become embodied in him as a social instinct. Thus, to quote Mr. Spencer's own words, "The experiences of utility, organized and consolidated through all past generations of the human race, have been producing corresponding nervous modifications, which, by continued transmission and accumulation, have become in us certain faculties of moral intuition, certain emotions responding to right and wrong conduct, which have no apparent basis in the individual experiences of utility." [1]

But there are manifold experiences of utility, such as the more immediate means of gratifying the appetites, cases of prudence and economy, industry, etc., which have been subject to all this accumulation and organization as much as any others, but which have not been transformed into moral intuitions. Why this difference? It is due, according to Mr. Spencer, to the fact that the earlier and simpler feelings, which refer to more immediate

[1] Data of Ethics, p. 123.

gratifications, have been found by the accumulated experience of the race not to be as highly conducive to welfare as guidance by feelings more complex, concerned with more indirect and remote and more widely diffused effects. The later evolved, more compound and more representative feelings, serving as they do to adjust the conduct to more distant and general needs and greater benefits in the end, come to have authority; and the lower and simpler feelings, as less conducive to ultimate benefit, are by comparison looked upon as without authority.[1]

It is evident, then, how action under such sentiments as love, justice, truth, should become especially valuable and honored. But conduct of this kind is recognized by the moral sense as something more. It is not merely a dictate of prudence to be kind, equitable, and trustful, but something that we feel *bound* to do, something that we *ought*. Whence this imperative character and sense of coercive-

[1] Data of Ethics, pp. 114, 122, 126.

ness, which is the most striking characteristic of a moral duty?

This originates, says Mr. Spencer, "from experience of those several forms of restraint that have established themselves in the course of civilization, — the political, religious, and social." [1]   The punishments which they severally have inflicted in the past, or the dread of legal, supernatural, or social penalty which our ancestors have felt, have become ingrained by inheritance in us, forming an inner compulsion, born with us, restraining us from immediate and present gratifications, such as those upon which political, religious, and social penalties have been laid, and urging us by a sort of nervous reverberation of our ancestors' fears to pursue those more remote and general ends which these external powers have generally favored.

The sentiment of moral obligation is thus due, in the main, according to Mr. Spencer,[2] to fears of political, social, and religious pen-

[1] Data of Ethics, p. 126.   [2] Ibid., pp. 115–127.

alties. The general sense of duty disengages itself gradually from these other controls; an abstract idea is formed of it; and, as often occurs in the case of abstract ideas, acquires " an illusive independence." [1]   But as the moral motive becomes more distinct and predominant, it loses its associated consciousness of coercion and begins to fade. " The sense of duty or moral obligation is transitory, and will diminish as fast as moralization increases." [2] " This self-compulsion, which at a relatively high stage becomes more and more a substitute for compulsion from without, must itself, at a still higher stage, practically disappear." [3]

Such, in brief, is Mr. Spencer's now famous theory of the origin of moral ideas and sentiments. At the first glance we cannot fail to see its utter inconsistency with the received principles of ethics, and it seems to me to be in blank contradiction to our moral consciousness. The idea of duty is granted only an

---

[1] Data of Ethics, p. 125.
[2] Ibid. p. 127.   [3] Ibid. p. 130.

" illusive independence." The Categorical Imperative, to use Kant's classic term, instead of being recognized as the voice of a legitimate authority, is but the cerebral vestige of our ancestors' alarms before the menace of social disgrace, the vengeance of some despot or dead chieftain's ghost. Our moral ideas represent, not what we individually see to be wise or right, but what preceding generations thought most useful. By the subtle operations of heredity these ideas of our ancestors as to what was conducive to their happiness have not only smuggled themselves into our brains, but have assumed a sacred authority. As the suggestion of a companion may take possession of the brain of a delirious person, and the thought and will of a hypnotizer seize control of the mind of his patient and make him do what his own reason and will would never order, so do the experiences of past generations as to the pleasurable and the painful obsess our brains with their illusory convictions of self-evident right and

solemn duty. Not only is our general idea
of duty an illusion, but our special ethical
ideas are hallucinations due, in more than
one case, to no superior wisdom of our ancestors, but simply to their superstitions. For
example, the *asceticism* which finds moral
worth in self-denial rather than self-enjoy-
ment, and which repudiates the idea of happiness as the end of conduct, is derived by
Mr. Spencer from the devil-worship of the
savage and "the views of life and conduct
which originated with those who propitiated
deified ancestors by self-tortures." [1]

The perception of an ineradicable difference
between right and wrong, an inevitable obligation to obey the right, and a sense of sin
when we disobey it, have always formed the
basic elements of morality. "This instinct,"
eloquently says Isaac Taylor, "flushes in the
cheek of every sensitive child, and it prevails
over the laborious sophistications of the philosopher. This belief is cherished as an in-

[1] Data of Ethics, pp. 29, 40.

estimable jewel by the best and purest of human beings; it is bowed to in dismay by the foulest and the worst; its rudiments are a monition of eternal truth whispered in the ear of infancy; its articulate announcements are a dread fore-doom ringing in the ears of the guilty adult." In the analytical crucible of Mr. Spencer all these lofty, solemn, and essential elements of the moral sense are resolved into the common clay of the rest of our nature. Duty is in truth but prudence, and remorse the echo of our ancestors' chastisements. Conscience itself is but an evanescent phenomenon, due to the maladjustment of our nature (still in great measure retaining its military and anti-social constitution) to the industrial and social stage into which evolution has now passed. When the transition is fully made and the limit of evolution reached, conscience will disappear. Its place will be taken by organic necessity and an instinctive promotion of happiness.

The very statement of the theory would

seem enough to show its falsity; but its champions will demand specifications of error, based not upon the views they would over- throw, but upon grounds which they them- selves admit.

L ET us test Mr. Spencer's system, then, by that which in it constitutes a thing good or bad; namely, its consequences. Will it be likely to be conducive to the welfare of the race if universally adopted? Mr. Spencer has himself recognized the danger of a moral vacuum in society. One of the standing and urgent needs of society is that of a controlling moral agency. The very reason that led the author to hasten the composition and publication of the " Data of Ethics " in advance of its regular place in his synthetic system is that, as he says, " Few things can happen more disastrous than the decay and death of a regulative system no longer fit, before another and fitter regulative system has grown up to replace it." [1]   It is most proper to ask, then, whether Mr. Spencer's ethical system is capa-

[1] Data of Ethics, Preface, p. iv.

ble of providing the needed moral regulation for humanity. Does it possess the requisite authority to give it efficiency in controlling mankind, supposing that it should become generally adopted?

It seems to me that it does not. Were men already perfectly evolved in their moral nature so that whatever it was right for them to do they would take satisfaction in doing, the new ethics would of course suffice, for no control at all would then be needed; but it will be many ages yet before that moral Utopia will be reached. Meantime, man needs a system that can compel him to do what he does not find personally agreeable. Any system of ethics that is to be efficacious must have some law-giving power that may keep the lower nature subordinate to the higher, and not allow the general happiness to be sacrificed to personal and selfish gratifications. What power of this kind has Mr. Spencer's ethics?

Mr. Spencer aims to show us that a true morality represents the ultimate stage of evolution, and reproduces in social life that permanent equilibration toward which every form of evolution constantly tends, and in which the self-regarding impulses shall be harmonized with the social impulses. Its disciples are invited to act in such ways as may bring posterity as promptly as possible to this happy goal.

If a man's interests coincide with the helping forward of this movement, he will naturally aid it. But if he is called upon to sacrifice his own particular interests to this coming social perfection of posterity, will he not be likely to say, What has posterity ever done for me that I should make myself wretched for it? "The man," it has well been said, " who does not already love his contemporaries whom he has seen, is unlikely to love them the more for the sake of a remote posterity whom he will never see at all." [1]

Evolutionary ethics, to be sure, bids its disciples guide themselves by the higher, more

[1] Westminster Review, January, 1883, p. 63.

complex, and universal feelings. But why ?. Only because they are directed towards wider benefit, are more conducive to general happiness. Its only motive to induce a man to speak the truth or to act honestly and benevolently is *prudence,* — a consideration of the ultimate advantage of self and others. But suppose the man says, "I prefer my immediate and personal advantage. By honesty I may possibly do better in the end ; but by cheating, I know I do better now. A bird in the hand is worth two in the bush. If my cheating should not turn out as well in the end, I am quite willing to stand the cost of it for the sake of the present gain." What argument can the ethical scheme which we are considering bring to bear on such a man ?

To see the fatal lack of authority inherent in the Spencerian ethics, let us take a concrete case and consider it more fully. Let us suppose that one of Mr. Spencer's disciples, whose moral nature is a little unfortunate in its inheritance of a surplus of egoism over altruism, has just found a mislaid deed which proves that the home in which he is living is not his, but belongs to a rich neighbor. In accordance with the egoistic nature which he has inherited, he has made up his mind quietly to destroy the deed and keep the unjustly held estate. Mr. Spencer, happening to visit him, is informed of the circumstance, and at once proceeds to remonstrate with him. On what grounds could he remonstrate, and what defences could the disciple bring forth from Mr. Spencer's own system? The dialogue, I think, would run something as follows : —

Mr. Spencer. To destroy this deed, sir, as you propose, would be very wrong.

Disciple. Why so?

Mr. S. The estate belongs to your neighbor. You have no right to diminish his happiness.

Disciple. I shall not do so. He has already more property than he can manage with comfort; whereas its loss would make me and my invalid wife and child miserable, perhaps kill them. The act conduces to a greater aggregate of happiness to self and others, and therefore, as you have shown us, must be right.

Mr. S. You forget, sir, that I told you that the aggregate of happiness was not to be directly estimated, neither was it to be immediately aimed at, but that it was to be best gained by observing the unchanging conditions of welfare, chief among which is justice.

Disciple. How do you know that justice is so essential to general welfare, if it is impossible to estimate pains and pleasures correctly?

Mr. S. Does not your own conscience tell you?

Disciple. As you have shown, the voice of conscience is a humbug, pretending to a divinity which it has no right to; the idea of duty as distinct from prudence has, as you have told us, only an "illusive independence." Its throne was usurped and its regalia fabricated by the arts of that tricksy sprite, "Association." We owe no obedience to such a pretender. Conduct, in every case, is a question simply of prudence or imprudence; nothing more.

Mr. S. At any rate the voice of conscience is the accumulated experience of the past; and that ought to warn you of the bad results of injustice.

Disciple. You have yourself taught me how far I stand above the past, how superstitious and unenlightened men were in the old times. I will not believe, and do not think you yourself believe, that our ancestors, in their ignorance and barbarism, knew more about right and wrong, or how better to secure the welfare of myself and others, than the reason of a modern man may perceive, especially one whose mind has been illuminated by the great truths of evolution. I have always been taught to think that a man was to determine what was right for him by his own reason, not by the opinion of others. In more than one place you have spoken, in a very caustic tone, of those who think that social opinion constitutes right. But if the social opinion of our generation cannot make or unmake right, how can the social opinions of past generations? I do not think that you will claim, yourself, that we ought to accept all the moral ideas of our ancestors. Have you not told us in your "Data of Ethics"[1] that the supremacy of higher feelings is only to be "a qualified supremacy," and that the authority of the lower and simpler feelings, though ordinarily less than that of the higher and more compound, is "occasionally greater"?

Mr. S. Well, yes; now you remind me of it. And I have also intimated that these innate perceptions of right may possibly have to be corrected as to their form, and must be "duly enlightened and made precise by an analytic intelligence."[2]

---

[1] Pages 111 and 112.
[2] Data of Ethics, pp. 167 and 173.

Disciple.   That is just what I have done in this case.

Mr. S.   But no analysis can make injustice a better rule than justice.   Justice is the general and standard means for the attainment of happiness, special and general, and it should therefore be the proximate aim.

Disciple.   Yes.   As you say, it is a *means*, but happiness is the *end*.   And the securing of the end is always paramount to the use of the means.   Right and wrong, as you have told us, vary with the environment. The family circumstances that form my environment in this instance demand a modification of the general rule.   If I should act with regard to justice alone in this case, and give up the estate, I should impoverish myself and my family, and render all of us miserable for the rest of our lives.   Now, as you have pointed out in your book called " The Study of Sociology," [1] speaking of a

------

[1] Page 277.

similar case, that of the pursuit of liberty, "The worth of the means must be measured by the degree in which this end is achieved. A citizen nominally having complete means, but partially securing the end, is less free than another who uses incomplete means to more purpose." So I say with reference to the means "justice" and "injustice" in reference to the end "happiness." Injustice is in this case the better means, as it better secures the surplus of pleasure over pain, which is the supreme good. Nay, in your "Data of Ethics"[1] you have said the same thing in as many words. "If the rules of right living are those of which the total results, individual and general, direct and indirect, are most conducive to human happiness, then it is *absurd* to *ignore the immediate results* and recognize only the remote results." Now, the immediate results in this case have one voice. They unanimously bid me destroy the proof that this estate belongs

[1] Page 95.

to any one else, as the surest and quickest
way of preserving the happiness of myself
and my family, and also of my weary neighbor, already too much burdened with great
possessions.

Mr. S. But if all men should act in this
way, society would suffer badly. Justice is
the very cement of social order, and your
unjust act will tend to dissolve the mutual
confidence and general integrity which alone
allow society, with all its higher employments,
to flourish.

Disciple. Do not be disturbed. I shall
not advertise what I do. Nobody but you
and I will know it. There will be little
or no chance for it to produce imitators
or to affect the conduct and future acts of
others. I am but an obscure individual,
and the effect of my example would be but
small, if it were known; and as I intend
to keep it a profound secret, there will be
no evil effects worth mentioning to come
from it. Certainly, the remote evil effects

will not begin to outweigh the immediate good effects to myself and family. The "surplus" will be most decidedly a "surplus of pleasure," and, therefore, the action will be right.

Mr. S. You forget that I have taught you that nothing is perfectly right if it gives pain to any one, and this proposition sadly shocks me.

Disciple. True, it is not absolutely right; hardly anything, as you have shown, can be, which man does in his present unfortunate environment and imperfectly evolved stage. But if I should give up the estate to its true owner, that would not be completely right; for, as you have shown, "actions are completely right only when, besides being conducive to future happiness, special and general, they are immediately pleasurable."[1] As it is inevitable that my action should be partially wrong in any case, I prefer to secure the immediate and

[1] Data of Ethics, p. 99.

personal pleasure that I can make sure of, rather than aim at the more remote and uncertain returns which regard for the general welfare may bring.

Mr. S. I regret to see you so absorbed in egoistic satisfaction, and so forgetful of the altruistic sympathies that should impel you to the other-regarding actions without which society cannot evolve.

Disciple. You forget that you have yourself told us, and at some considerable length have "clearly shown," that "pure altruism is suicidal," and that "egoism precedes altruism in order of imperativeness,"[1] and that altruism is rather to be diminished in its sphere, than increased, as society evolves towards a complete development.[2] I am not only convinced of it, but I intend to act on these principles whenever I can gain anything for myself by so doing.

(*Mr. Spencer walks off, looking very grave, and repeating to himself a sentence from his*

[1] Data of Ethics, p. 197.   [2] Ibid., p. 251.

"*Study of Sociology:*" "*A utilitarian system of ethics cannot at present be rightly
thought out even by the select few, and is
quite beyond the mental reach of the many.*")

To drop our illustration, and return to
straightforward statement, I look upon the
teachings of the "Data of Ethics," if they
should be generally adopted and put into
practice, as fraught with disastrous consequences to the morals of society.

Not only does Mr. Spencer's own careful
and guarded exposition of the principles of
the new ethics supply ample defences for
selfish dishonesty and violence, but the fundamental principles of his system, when
pushed onward by more rigorous reasoners,
sweep forward into the bluntest contradic-
tions of all received morality. We have
already noticed the logical inconsistencies
between Mr. Spencer's retention of our intuitions of justice as moral guides and authorities, and the rest of his system.

Later and more audacious champions of the

evolution of morals would eliminate these
ideas of the just as an excrescence on the body
of naturalistic ethics. A striking instance of
this may be found in Mr. Wordsworth Donisthorpe's recent book on "Individualism." In
his inquiry as to its basis, he discusses very
frankly the question of the justification of laws
and the foundation of civil rights. Mr.
Spencer seems to him altogether too finical and
too timid; and he boldly throws off all
disguises and avows the naked conclusions of
the evolutionist premises. "The all-sufficient
warrant," he maintains, "for any effective
governing power in a social group doing whatever it thinks best, is the welfare of the group."
He ridicules the idea of the minority of the
members, or, for that matter, the majority, if
they are stupid, or poor, or ill-organized, having
any natural and inalienable rights. So-called
rights are the results of a trial of strength.
"Right is transfigured might." [1] What is
called justice is only an economical compromise

[1] Page 263.

of contending forces, or the illegitimate interference of paternal despotism from sympathy for the under-dog in the fight.

The maxim Mr. Donisthorpe commends is the maxim of the anarchist: "Let him take who hath the power; let him keep who can. That is property, is it not?" But what is to prevent the strong from robbing the weak? "Suppose the many, it will be asked, finding themselves poor, take it into their heads to expropriate the few, what then?" "Well, why not?" Mr. Donisthorpe replies. "If it can be shown that the robbery of the rich can be effected, and effected with advantage to the poor, I cannot see, for the life of me, why it should not be done. It is contrary to morality? But, unfortunately, highfaluting abstractions butter no parsnips. Besides, I deny it. Morality is co-extensive with self-interest. If anybody disputes that, he is wrong. It is rude and dogmatic of me to say so, but it is a short answer, and I am not going to discuss the first principles of ethics here. I repeat emphatically, if the poor and many can see their way to dispossessing the rich and few, and to reap advantage from the process, then they have a right and a duty to do it." [1]

Now these are no wild words from the mouth of some starved or freezing outcast of society, or some half-crazed anarchist maddened by the sufferings and wrongs he has endured; they are the frankly announced results, as to natural moral rights, of an evolutionist scholar and writer, in an elaborate and carefully written book.

I think. it must be evident, then, what a fatal lack of authority the Spencerian system of Ethics would have in compelling a well-posted disciple to do an act of duty opposed to his immediate interest, or to yield any selfish advantage of which he could cling hold.

Suppose, then, that the theory be universally accepted, and that generation after generation

[1] Page 257.

grow up under it. In a century or two, when heredity and the new moral education had done their work, what would be left of conscience? According to Mr. Spencer, our sense of duty has been built up by association and heredity into an illusive sovereignty and sacred authority quite different from the experiences of utility out of which it proceeded. When this artificial origin is generally known, may not association and heredity now tend to tear down again their work?

As M. Guyau, the keen French critic whose early death was such a loss to the world of letters, pointed out in his able work on " La Morale anglaise contemporaine," [1] is it not very doubtful if the moral sense would continue to perform its functions as before when the "illusiveness" of these current moral sanctions is comprehended, and the manner in which these ethical hallucinations have been engendered is thoroughly ventilated among intelligent people?

[1] Livre iii. chapitre iv.

Let us look at the effect of reason and will upon hallucinations, and the conduct of those under their influence, as shown to us by physiology and psychology.

In hallucination there are two kinds,— the unconscious and the conscious. The latter is much the more easy to dissipate. Now, moral beings (those fortunately deluded creatures who fancy that the cerebral vestiges of their ancestors' alarms are signs of personal responsibility, and that their inherited reminiscences of their predecessors' utilitarian experiences are direct intuitions of eternal truths, whose authority is higher than all considerations of advantage or disadvantage) belong at present to the class of the unconsciously hallucinated.

But when men shall have been instructed in the new ethics, and have firmly adopted it, their delusion will be turned to a conscious one. The voice of conscience will still, for a time, at least, according to the well-known law of survival, speak within the breast.

Remorse will still gnaw the heart of the transgressor. But will these illusions then be
likely to retain their vividness and power
when it is discovered that they are not true
representations of present realities, but results
of certain nervous derangements transmitted
from ancient time ? They may mirror certain
phenomena of former days, and they may be
useful for the protection of those around ; but
they do not represent truly the present and
personal circumstances of the man himself, nor
what is most useful for him in his individual
circumstances. Thus, as fast as men, adopting
the new ethics, satisfy themselves of the illusiveness of duty as an innate and independent
fact, its irresistible force over the will will
be lost, and if enough of the sentiment still
exists to render them uneasy, they will turn
to such pleasures and distractions as may
palliate and eventually silence it altogether.

But the moral faculty, it will be said, is not
merely a collection of moral ideas which may
be crowded out by a new set of ideas, it is

an organic structure wrought out by the work of generations. As it has not risen in a day it will not pass away in a day; and the alarms of the old school of moralists are unfounded.

To a certain extent this is true; but the breakwater against the full effect of the new ethics which is furnished by this fact can only last for a comparatively short time after the new moral theory has become generally adopted. It is, of course, a groundless expectation to look to see men and women in whom the moral nature has been well developed under the old system, *at once* rush into unbridled selfishness and sensuality upon their acceptance of the new system. Men's theories often have very slight connection with or control over, their habits; and it is their habits, their organized character, which is the spring from whence the life-currents of action flow.

But when a belief which has been recognized as the most authoritative over a man's life comes to be looked upon as only an hallucination, it cannot pass away without more or less influence over the discharges of his will and the intensity and direction of his moral life. Though some organic derangement project again and again upon our vision some spectral image, though some mental disorder, such as melancholia, fill our minds with mental delusions of loss of strength or property, yet if the patient can be made to recognize that these *are delusions*, then the power of thought will correct the false perception, the consciousness of the genuine facts will react upon the nervous centres, neutralizing the organic trouble and bringing about a cure of the sick organ.

So will it be, as M. Guyau so well argues, with the sense of obligation and of remorse for sin when men become fully persuaded that instead of corresponding to eternal laws of right and retribution, these ideas and sentiments are but metaphysical chimeras which have fraudulently assumed the robe of divine avengers, — that they are, in truth, only altru-

istic tendencies and social instincts which
have been accumulated in our brain through
successive generations; that the supreme and
ultimate end of existence is to get happiness;
and that what we call virtue has no claim on
man unless it can secure him a surplus of
pleasure. When the consciousness is thus
enlightened, then both the moral pain and
the ethical illusions will soon disappear, until
the disordered moral faculty itself will, by
successive steps, adjust itself to the new intellectual consciousness. As long as a man
still practically grants to duty an authority
in opposition to which questions of mere
utility are to be disregarded; as long as he
feels remorse for his sin as a sin, not as a
mere blunder; as long as he leads his life
as one who has direct perceptions of eternal
moral distinctions, and with whom the utilitarian experiences of present and past ages
are equally without weight if opposed to these
moral insights, it is evident that he remains
not half-converted to the theory that he has

professedly adopted. The other instincts with which man was, like the animals, originally endowed, have for the most part been successively effaced, their place being taken and their work done by intelligence. The moral instinct, the only one left of whose meaning and origin we are still unconscious (except among advanced evolutionists), will also soon disappear through the onward march of philosophic and scientific enlightenment. Those who have emancipated themselves from the superstition of its divine constraint will calmly leave the work of self-sacrifice and painful discharge of the social obligations to those who still labor under the old hallucinations, and will quietly secure their own advantage by attending to their individual welfare.

As a matter of fact, there are not a few cases at the present day in which such an enfeebling and often entire disappearance of the moral instinct seems to be connected with just such causes and courses of reasoning. It is not indeed among the ordinary

class of criminals that this is found. The
ordinary criminal belongs to a species in whom
the flesh, not the mind, is predominantly
developed, and in whom, if the moral instinct
has perished, it has been suffocated by the
animal passions. " But there is another class
of criminals," as M. Guyau remarks, " the true
transgressors, who know what they do, who
are capable of reflection, who represent man
not merely physically imbruted, but morally
degraded. These are nothing else but sceptics
who practise their scepticism. Morality is
to them a chimera ; good and evil a preju-
dice. Every man follows his own interest,
and seeks it where he finds it. All men are
selfish, — in other ways than they, perhaps,
but in no less degree." So we might formulate the general thought which disengages
itself from the acts and words of this class ;
and this thought in its last analysis constitutes the primitive and essential basis of all
exclusively utilitarian doctrine. Hence, doubtless, as M. Guyau says, " that irony with

which certain criminals astonish us, that bitter raillery concerning ideal good ; hence comes that cynicism which sometimes touches stoicism, that perseverance in vice which sometimes implies courage, and thus appears as a distant image of perseverance in good, — in a word, that supreme affirmation in suffering and death that all is negation and nothingness."

Our trenchant critic may perhaps have overdrawn somewhat his picture of the rocks ahead of the new ethics. I would not for a moment credit the advocates of that theory with any sympathy with moral license, with the least desire to weaken or remove the restraints by which vice and crime are held in check. Especially unjust is any attempt to find a motive for the promulgation of this theory in the personal laxity of its advocates. They are men of earnest purpose, whose devotion to the pure truth without regard to consequences is only too thorough. Their misfortune is that they neither see how inconsistent this blind devotion is with their fundamental standard of the general welfare, nor will they open their eyes to see what fruit others are raising from the seed that they are planting. The evil tendencies as yet, of course, have had but little time to ripen. For more than one generation the ballast of the older morality will keep society comparatively steady. But when the influences of a new theory which manifestly lacks those more powerful sanctions and that constant appeal to the finer, nobler, and diviner part of humanity, which formed the glory and the strength of old-time righteousness, shall have come into general operation for several generations, then the maintenance of social health will become a grave problem. When the only sanction that is left to make a man submit to the requirements of the general good is his own interest, what hold will law and virtue have over such a man beyond the reach of the constable's club? If a man chooses to sacrifice his future good to his present, or the

good of his fellows to his own, what argument is left to morality with which to restrain
him ? When the claims of social duty are
analyzed into the preponderant surplus of
general happiness, as set over against the
small sum total of personal happiness, when
it is a mere balance of the selfish gratification
of many against the selfish gratification of
one, individuals everywhere will say : " Though
the surplus of general happiness is abstractly
a greater aggregate, yet my personal happiness is much more precious and of more
moment to *me*. What claim has society to
demand of me the sacrifice of my all, for
that which is a drop in the bucket in the
satisfaction of its general ends ? What right
has any opinion of a majority to restrain me
from seeking my own advantage in whatever
way I find most profitable for myself ? "

These questions are legitimate outcomes of
this philosophy, and if it is once adopted by
self-willed minds, will surely be asked and
acted upon.

If Mr. Spencer's theory of the origin of our sense of duty in the alarms and fears and constraints of preceding generations, and of the illusiveness of the independence and authority of conscience, are indeed true, then the worst thing that could happen for society is for this to become generally known. And as in Mr. Spencer's ethics the only test of what is right is its consequences in reference to the welfare of humanity, these injurious results of the system are not merely things that may well cause us to pause and consider, but they are logical inconsistencies, and ought properly to take away from all utilitarians any moral right (on their own ground) to diffuse them. To give moral health to society and to maintain the sway of righteousness there, higher and more independent sanctions than those of Mr. Spencer's system must be called into play. Those noblest and most needed virtues — steadfast integrity, purity, and unselfishness — are not to be enforced by considerations of " surplus of pleasure over pain." The returns of happiness, either special or general, for such virtues are too remote and uncertain to have much efficiency by themselves. It is only the unqualified supremacy of duty, and the authority of a conscience which is something more than an organic remembrance of our ancestors' experience, that can maintain these virtues and destroy the vices which are their opposites. An ethical system which, whatever regard it may profess for these authorities, will in practice destroy them, is plainly unfit to be taken as the regulative agency of human events. If nature or past experience had left us no stronger moral system than this, we should have had forthwith to invent one ourselves. Were such a system of ethics as Mr. Spencer's to be universally adopted, and should the poorer and more ignorant classes as well as the educated become familiar with its principles, the cloud of social anarchy would soon be lifting its black and ragged edge above the horizon.

BUT prophecies, it may be retorted here, are not arguments. They can be manufactured for the bolstering up of one side as easily as of the other. Human nature has an inherent conservatism, which manifests itself with greater power the more all external restraints are removed. Let us discuss the question, then, simply as a question of fact or probable truth.

Mr. Spencer's theory of the origin of the moral sentiments may seem to deprive them of authority. But is not the theory true? And if we have reason to think the theory true, is it not likely that, as all other truth, it will in practice not be deleterious, but beneficial, to man?

Let us examine the theory, then, on its merits, as presenting or not a satisfactory origin of conscience and our intuitive moral perceptions and sentiments.

What are the proofs of the theory? Mr. Spencer vouchsafes no arguments in its support. He simply states his explanation as carrying its own proof with it, and calmly ignores the many objections which naturally suggest themselves.

Perhaps he believes that Mr. Darwin has argued the matter at sufficient length in his "Descent of Man." At any rate, the grounds on which his theory rests are to be gathered by the implications of his explanation. These appear to be, —

1. The general law of evolution, everywhere producing the more complex from the more simple.

2. The testimony of history that moral ideas are not found in the early ages in that purity and fulness that characterize them now, but that they are found to emerge gradually, increasing in delicacy and elevation with the growth of culture and the experiences of the race.

3. The established effects of association and heredity, accumulating, infusing, and transmuting experiences.

4. The special analogy of the derivation of our ideas of space and time from organized and consolidated experience.

5. The coincidence that feelings are called moral in proportion as they are representative instead of simple, and concerned with indirect, remote, and general effects, rather than direct, near, and special (chapter vii.).

Now, in reply, I affirm that there is nothing in the idea of evolution (within the range that that idea is supported by the facts of life and the universe) that requires any such origin for our moral nature. Grant that in the early ages moral ideas are not found in that completeness that characterizes them now, but that they are found to emerge gradually, increasing in purity and elevation with the experience of the race and the growth of culture. Grant that, as we go back, we not only find the moral element more limited and obscure, but that if we were able to trace back man's pedigree far enough, we should come to a period when man (if such a supposed semi-brutal ancestor would deserve to be called man) did not possess a moral consciousness, but only the simpler feelings of pleasure and pain, advantage and disadvantage.

But because these experiences of utility may have preceded moral ideas and led up to them, it by no means follows that these experiences of the useful have *produced* the moral ideas. Antecedents are not necessarily causes, nor are conditions to be confounded with sources. While the moral faculty, as I maintain, is original and independent, and moral ideas undecomposable, it is nevertheless quite natural that a long process of mental development should be required before man could apprehend fully these moral ideas. As with all other *à priori* ideas, they arise only on occasion of experience and emerge involved in that experience. Man's experiences of pleasure and pain for generations may

11

thus have supplied the requisite conditions
by which the thoughts of man were so elevated that at length the eternal stars of moral
truth, before below the horizon, at last
came within the field of vision. But because
of this, to argue that the moral sentiments
are but transmuted products of the experiences of utility, would be a most evident
non sequitur. One might as well argue that
when father and grandfather, in the midst of
a Fourth of July crowd, lift the young heir
of the family upon their shoulders to give
him a sight of the fireworks, the pyrotechnic
spectacle that bursts upon the boy's gaze
is merely a changed form of the muscular
strain of his progenitors, the contraction of
their sinews being concentrated and transformed into his optic vibrations.

The influences of our experiences of utility
may account for man's ascent into the field
of vision where ethical principles come into
view, they may account for the opening of
the moral eye, the emergence of the latent

moral sentiments, or the more perfect application of moral ideas as culture progresses; but the *germ* of the moral faculty, the fundamental notions of a difference between right and wrong, and an obligation to do the one and evade the other, must have been present at the very beginning of moral life, at the outset of that rational and conscious existence which constitutes the distinctive element of humanity.

Starting then with such a moral germ, however small or vague, we may consistently imagine all our various ethical sentiments and ideas as growing up from it. As soon as the struggle for existence becomes conscious of itself in the reason of a thinking being, he must not only feel the instincts of self-defence, but also, as those instincts unfold their implications to his reason, he must think, " I have a *right* to this life and self of mine." And as he met others of his own species and discerned their likeness to himself, he would transfer to his idea of them whatever attributes he had become conscious of as belonging to himself. As he was vividly convinced of his own right to life, he would recognize a similar right in them. By this recognition living together becomes possible, and social life henceforth can start on its career. The various other instincts of man, such especially as the reproductive, maternal, and social, as they become conscious, disengage the sense of right bound up with them. As the power of abstract thought increases and sympathy strengthens, these ideas of right and *not* right are extended to all kinds of feelings, purposes, and personal and social relations.

But it is only through the germ of the moral notion present from the first with man (though very likely in only an inchoate form) that man's experience can give rise to this moral evolution. The idea of the rightfulness of any class of acts, such as the just or the beneficent, instead of being subsequent to and derived from an experience of the usefulness of such acts through several generations, may much more rationally be considered to be the more simple and primary perception.

As maternal instinct was antecedent to any consciousness of its use, so the moral instincts preceded any recognition of the advantages attendant upon exercising them. Before man ever got so far as to reason that the preservation of his life would be conducive to a surplus of happiness either special or general, he felt the impulse to preserve it, and moreover felt that he had a right to preserve it, and stood up in the strength of righteous indignation against those who would rob him of his own.

Instead of gregarious life engendering morality in that hitherto unmoral creature, the primitive man, as the evolutionist school suppose, it was rather, as I conceive, the moral instincts, more or less developed in man, that held social life together, and in fact made it possible. The evolutionists talk of increase of numbers forcing men to live together, and thus compelling and producing higher morality, in a way that ignores altogether the distinctive nature of man as a factor having aught to do with the result. They talk as if they thought that any other species, say the race of tigers, if only kept herded together long enough and closely enough, would evolve a love of justice and a care for the welfare of their fellows such as has been developed in man.

They would simply have torn each other to pieces. That the human race has not, but has flourished and risen the more, the closer it has been pressed together, is due not so much to that pressure and contiguity, as rather to the different nature, the germs of a moral constitution preparing him for society, which formed his original endowment.

The same is the case with the origin of the idea of justice. Before man's experience had begun to enable him to draw any such generalization as that "justice is more conducive to the general happiness than injustice," man must have recognized a spirit of fair and equal dealing between man and man as plainly the fit and proper thing. Mr. Spencer himself has shown in his criticism of Bentham that "justice is a more intelligible notion," [1] and more fit as an end, than happiness.

He also asserts (what travellers corroborate) that among primitive men an approach to the conception of justice is traceable, and that among the early races who have given their thought literary form there was quite a distinct conception of justice.

It would have been well, in this and many other cases, if Mr. Spencer could have remembered in his evolutionary theorizing, the simple truths with which he confutes the great utilitarian teacher of the last century. We might then have been spared such an inconsistency as he exhibits when he presents the moral sentiments, such as honesty, truthfulness, and justice, for example,[2] as more complex, re-representative, and later-evolved no-

---

[1] Data of Ethics, pp. 164, 165.   [2] Ibid., pp. 107, 123.

tions, directed to more "distant, involved, and diffused effects," and derives from *these* qualities their superior moral worth. How these qualities could endow them with any *authority*, especially that overmastering power that the higher duties have, driving us to the end they ordain, in spite of physical pain, family opposition, or social disgrace, is something that passes comprehension.

Our idea of duty, according to Mr. Spencer, is a subjective echo, transmuted by thé wondrous chemistry of "association" and "heredity" from ancestral experiences of pain and pleasure.

Now, as any memory of a long past experience, however well preserved, is much less vivid than the experience itself, so this organized memory of our ancestors' feelings (if that is all that the approval or reproval of conscience really is) ought to be still more dim and faint.

On the contrary, these moral emotions sweep over the mind with a power before which all other considerations of pain or pleasure have to yield.

There is nothing in the complexity, the generality, or the "lateness of evolution" of these ideas, or their remote, diffused effects, that explains this unparalleled power and sovereignty of moral ideas. Were the source of them to be found in these qualities which Mr. Spencer presents, our other abstract ideas and philosophical general sentiments ought to enjoy the same sacred character, for they are equally late, re-representative, and general in their effects. It is not, in fact, any of these qualities that give to truth, justice, and honesty their moral sovereignty, but simply the ease, directness, and certainty with which our moral intuitions perceive the quality of rightness in them.

May we then find the source of moral authority in the immense duration of time during which association and heredity have been accumulating and consolidating these experiences of utility which at last are trans-

formed into ethical intuitions ? So most
of Mr. Spencer's disciples, whose zeal has
generally been in inverse ratio to their knowledge of his system, have supposed. They
have presented the truth of the moral intuitions as guaranteed by the whole experience
of the human race behind them.

But, on the contrary, the feelings that,
according to Mr. Spencer, are the primitive
and ancient ones are the animal impulses
and egoistic sentiments, warlike passions, hate
of the stranger, sensual appetites, and pro-
miscuous gratifications of the lusts of the
body, — precisely, in short, the feelings and
habits to which we do *not* assign any virtuous character at all, but in great part the
reverse. The sentiments and habits that we
honor as virtues, such as love of our neighbor, conjugal fidelity, chastity, peaceableness,
and self-control, are those which Mr. Spencer
tells us have been only *lately* evolved, and
which have prevailed merely since the time
when industrial activities took the place of

the predatory life of man. Now, if the experience of the race, accumulated and consolidated through the much longer period of predatory life, the thousands or hundreds of thousands of years (as evolutionist *savants* reckon this period) during which man was slowly working through barbarism up to the industrial and peaceful stage, has not endowed our egoistic sentiments and sensual appetites with any moral authority, how comes it that the much briefer period of experience which humanity has had with the altruistic sentiments, and such habits as truth, chastity, and conjugal fidelity, should have given them such unquestionable obligation?

It is evident, then, that it is not the early nor the late evolution of sentiments, it is not the length or the brevity of the hereditary accumulation of experiences of their utility that gives feelings moral obligation.

In a race like the Scandinavian, that emerged from the predatory life little more than a thousand years ago, the sense of moral obligation is as strong as, if not even stronger than, in a race like the Chinese, that has been in the industrial stage for over four thousand years.

Some other explanation must be sought for the authority of the moral sentiments. Is it supplied, then, by that favorite resort of all rejecters of the intuitive theory, the power of association ?

Let us recall, in the first place, that the evolutionists themselves tacitly admit, by their rejection of the older hedonism, and their addition of heredity to the transforming forces, that "association" of itself is not sufficient.

But they suppose that when association and heredity unite their forces, and the combined pressure of political, social, and religious fears are applied through several generations of industrial and orderly life, that the transmutation of experiences of utility into convictions of duty somehow takes place. Is this a fact of observation ? Not at all.

It is simply an hypothesis. Has it been verified? Again, it must be acknowledged that it has not. Why are we to believe it then? Only on the ground of the general hypothesis of evolution and a few analogous occurrences.

We have seen that the general hypothesis of evolution does not require it. Let us glance at the analogies, and see if they and the natural effects of such an origin are such as to demand belief in it. The analogies especially relied upon are the formation of the intuition of space from organized and consolidated experience of our ancestors, and the manner in which habits and capacities, like those in music and art, or the habit of retrieving in dogs, consciously and laboriously acquired in one generation, become easy and, as it were, instinctive in the next. The first class of experience here referred to, it is to be observed, is unconscious experience which becomes conscious; the second, conscious experience transformed into unconscious instincts. To which kind of transmutation are we to liken this change of experiences of utility into moral sentiments, and the faculty of distinguishing right and wrong ?

Those of the evolutionist school who adduce as corroboration of the theory the cases of inherited habits in animals and special aptitudes in men, derived from certain acquired forms of knowledge or skill in their ancestors, evidently look upon the formation of the moral faculty as a case of conscious experience which has become unconscious. Mr. Spencer himself has not abstained from using language which has led both disciples and critics to understand him as holding this view.

But it is evident that this view — namely, that man's conscious inductions of the pleasures resulting from certain actions, and the pains accruing from others, and the habits resultant therefrom, have consolidated by inheritance into such moral sentiments and sense of duty as man possesses — is open to insuperable objections.

In the first place, such a supposed descent of the ethical stream from the higher plane of conscious induction or perception. of the useful in former generations to the lower plane of instinctive inclination or aversion to it in later generations, runs counter to the general law of evolutional production.

In the normal sequence of evolution, as the evolutionists have shown at length, the lower comes first, the higher afterwards. The instinctive and unconscious prepare the way for the reflective and conscious, and grow up to them; not *vice versa*.

When a higher stage has been once reached, there may then be reaction upon the lower, and the conscious may repeat itself in the unconscious. But it is not thus that new and higher elements are for the first time reached.

In the second place, intuitions such as our primary moral notions are not transmissible by heredity; for heredity, as Professor Bascom points out, [1] is a law of the organic realm, and operates in organic structures; and modifications, however great, like artificial disablement, that do not work into physiological structure, do not transmit themselves. The more conscious and voluntary our acquisitions are, the less are they transmitted by inheritance. The bequests that our nature receives from the conscious experience of former generations do not come in the form of conscious ideas or knowledge such as constitute our moral intuitions, but in the form of instinctive habits, blind inclinations, or aversions to the practice of certain acts. In a young pointer dog, for example, there is the impulse to point, but not discernment of what should be done. In the youth who inherits a musical organization there is inclination to music, and delight in it amounting perhaps to a positive fascination, but there is no knowledge of it. Heredity thus supplies habits, predispositions, automatic

[1] Comparative Psychology, chapter vii.

reproduction of movements; but it does not give ideas nor those highest operations of reason that we call intuitions.

But we need not argue more against this view of the origin of our moral sentiments. Mr. Spencer himself has explicitly denied that it is the view he holds, and has been most anxious that the objections to this theory of the derivation of morals, so effectively presented by Mr. Hutton, should be recognized as not applying to his theory. It is from the unconscious experiences of our race, from the vague, voluminous waves of pain or pleasure excited by varied instances of conduct tending to the benefit or detriment of the tribe, not from definite perceptions of utility or the conscious generalizations of the reflective reason, that our moral sentiments have been derived.

Now, what are the probabilities that support such a view? In the first place, let us take the analogous case by which Mr. Spencer would corroborate his theory. It is the case of the formation of our space intuitions from our organized experiences of touch. But this is itself a mere hypothesis, and needs proof and corroboration as much as the hypothesis it is adduced to confirm. It is very far from being generally accepted.

In the second place, it may be asked, if social approbation and disapprobation, accumulated and transmuted by heredity, becomes moral intuition, why then have not customs, like the eating of pork among Hebrews and Mussulmans, or the veiling of women in Oriental countries, which all these same forces of heredity, association, and social displeasure have now for generations been working on, been transformed into innate moral intuitions as sacred as justice, and as sure to reappear in a youth with this hereditarily tinged blood in him (no matter what other society or civilization he should be reared in) as any of the moral perceptions? Yet we know this does not take place.

If it be objected that there is a lack of real

and universal utility in such customs that may account for the difference, and that it is only the general conditions of social welfare which evolve into consciousness in the cerebral organism which they shape, and there assume sovereignty, then I would ask a further question, most undeniably pertinent. It is this: Why is it that only *certain* ones out of the many conditions of social welfare have become invested with the sanctions of morality, while other conditions, equally useful and equally constant in their operations on man (such as most of the laws of political economy, for instance), have not emerged as moral intuitions and acquired ethical sanction, instead of having only recently been discovered by the most advanced minds?

How is it, if this theory of Mr. Spencer's is true, that the special callings favoring civilization — that is, agriculture and manufacture — have never been considered virtues, nor a hunting life been reckoned vicious? How is it that celibacy has not been ranked as a sin, and that avarice and moderate personal pleasure-taking (both of them things beneficial to social welfare) should never have been reckoned as moral excellences?

Again, let us observe another significant fact; namely, that the habits of action and predispositions to do certain things, which heredity affords, are, in other cases than moral cases, stronger than our comprehension of what should be done. But in our moral constitution it is the reverse. Our habits are weaker than our insight; our footsteps lag behind our vision. The sad words of Ætias, —

> "Video meliora proboque,
> Deteriora sequor,"

constitute the universal lament of the sensitive conscience.

The injunctions of conscience do not run with the stream of our hereditary tendencies, but rather against them. It is not the acts to which we are predisposed by birth and association on which conscience usually puts its sanction, but rather those to which we are indisposed. The constant task of the moral faculty is precisely this, — by its categorical imperative to compel us, in the teeth both of our calculations of interest and our inherited inclinations, to walk the narrow path of duty. This *coercive* power of the moral faculty over our native predilections, to use Mr. Spencer's term, is one of the most marked features of human nature. It is not the characteristic of the most timid natures, as it would be if a mere cerebral reverberation of the political, social, or religious fears of our ancestors, but it especially distinguishes the manliest of men.

Now, in this superior development of our moral intuitions compared with our moral practice, and in this location of the moral emphasis, not upon those actions that heredity has prepared us to do, but upon those in regard to which our hereditary impulses are deficient, there is insurmountable refutal of the theory that this moral faculty is the product of heredity.

CHAPTER XI.

THESE considerations, it seems to me, ought to be decisive against Mr. Spencer's theories. But there is another phenomenon equally difficult of explanation on this basis. This is the idea of continued social progress as a duty, after the crust of inherited custom has once formed over the surface of society.

If Mr. Spencer's theory of the origin of duty be correct, how is it possible for civilization and liberty still to advance, after morality has once become predominant, without a moral cataclysm? According to the "Data of Ethics," moral ideas are but the distant echo of the past. How then can society be other than rigidly immobile? Or if there is progress, must it not be by the immoral, not the moral, that that progress is to be made?

Evidently, it would be firmly anchored to that past in all moral affairs. All the tremendous power of the moral sentiments would be working to keep humanity in the old ruts. The experiences of our ancestors as to what was beneficial or detrimental to them, according to the new ethics, have formed our social and mental structure, and our individual moral ideas are but functions of this structure. Those actions and opinions are right which bring a man into harmony with his environment, and so produce an aggregate of pleasurable effects for self and others.

Now, how was it possible, in accordance with this theory, for the transition to take place from that moral code in which militancy and egoism were sovereign, to that in which industrialism and altruism are paramount? Every variation toward this new method of conduct would expose itself to the condemnation of the old code as immoral; and natural selection, instead of furthering the survival

of such a new moral variation, would rather
tend to suppress it. Those of altruistic dis-
positions, those ready to bear others' burdens
or freely risk their lives for others, would, as
Darwin has admitted,[1] perish in larger number than meaner men, and often leave no
offspring to inherit their nobler nature.

So with later advances of morality, such as
the first attainment of high conceptions of
purity and truth, justice and a pure conscientiousness. These qualities are not, at
their first advent in an environment of lower
tone, conducive to the happiness of either
self or the others who are criticised and
reproved by these higher ideals. Entering
into an entirely inharmonious social environment, these qualities are sure to rasp and
disturb it. The reformer or saint who, with
any such too advanced ideal, breaks up painfully the comfortable course of society, society
will make smart for it. If the reformer

[1] Descent of Man, chap. v.

persists, society will most likely stone him
into an early grave. But painful and injurious
as this is to all concerned, the conscience
declares that this opposition to the social law,
in order to obey the inward voice, is the right
course, and the only right one. But if our
sense of right were but an organic registration
of society's past experience, our sense of duty
would rather urge us **to** conform to the **in-**
structions of that past experience, and passively
yield to that stream of ancestral habit in which
all about us drift along.

The fact that the enlightened conscience
recognizes an ideal right superior to all social
conventions, **to** which its loyalty is due, and
in faithfulness to which the man feels himself
bound **to resist his** hereditary impulses and
the social pressure about him, and **re-make**
both his inner and outer world, **as** far as he
can, in accordance **with** his vision of better
things; the **fact** that it is just this loyalty
to a higher **law, this** forward-looking, rather

than backward-looking gaze of conscience, that has given us all the moral progress that the world has seen, — these are phenomena that require for their explanation some less superficial theory than that expounded in the "Data of Ethics."

PART II.

THE POSITIVE RECONSTRUCTION OF ETHICS.

———◆———

CHAPTER I.

SUCH are the numerous and grave imper-
fections which exist, I believe, in Mr.
Spencer's effort to formulate the laws and
principles of ethics in the light of evolution. I
have tried to deal cautiously but candidly, and
to present no charge that was not weighty and
honestly based. But I think its deficiencies
are too many to justify it in receiving that
authority which, without such exposure, it will
be likely to receive, if not criticised as it
deserves.

What, then, would you have? it will doubtless be said. Do you expect, in the light of
modern progress, to erect at the boundaries of

ethics a sign inscribed with the autocratic prohibition, "Thus far shalt thou go and no farther, and here shall thy proud waves be stayed," and expect the rising tide of evolution to respect any such interdict?

Most surely not. I am neither so simple as to fancy that I, or any other critic, can play the part of Canute to the inrolling waves of evolution with any other result than discomfiture, nor have I any desire to play such a part if I could. I long ago adopted the evolution theory as a theory that is probably true; and I have been ready to accept it, and have myself applied it, not only in the realm of cosmology and biology, but in that of religion and morals. I believe that the principle of evolution has an important *rôle* to play in the field of ethics, and can throw much light and give valuable contribution to many of its vexed questions.

My concern is only that this great principle should be employed logically and thoroughly and wisely. Mr. Spencer's weakness is that he has used it chiefly in an inappropriate and contradictory fashion, drawing from it unreasonable and inconsistent conclusions.

What system of ethics, then, would you have us accept? If we are to walk in the light of evolution, can we go back to the shadows and obscurities of the abstract, *à priori* theories that reigned in former days?

That is equally far from my desire. We should go forward, rather, on the pathway that the great principle of evolution has opened for us. We should carry that principle through the whole domain of ethics with the consistent fidelity which in Mr. Spencer's "Data of Ethics" is so conspicuously lacking. We should not so engross ourselves with one class of evolutionary forces as to overlook entirely another, but should include all. We should trace the unfolding of morality, not merely, as Mr. Spencer does, just far enough back to damage our respect for it, and then stop, but go on to its ultimate and eternal roots, and thus restore to it its eternal sanctions;

and for the ultimate end and standard of
ethics we should not take that which is merely
an irregular incident and provisional instrument
of evolution, but we should adopt the same
noble goal toward which evolution itself is
plainly directing its course.

I would therefore essay to present a brief
outline of those ethical principles which it
seems to me the researches of modern knowledge and the great principles which they have
discovered, require. The basis of morality,
if it is to be reckoned more than a beautiful
dream, must be sought for in the facts of the
universe.

The old school of ethics when asked why
one ought not to hate or lie, replied,
" Because you ought not," and slammed
the door in the face of the inquirer. But the
school that is to meet the scientific demands
of our age must supply for ethics, as for
mechanics or æsthetics, a more rational ground.
If moral obligation is a reality at all, and not
a dream of idealists, a theological fiction

handed down by tradition, or a political expedient to keep the people in order, it must
be rooted in the nature of things.

Now, it is precisely here, I maintain, that
its ultimate source exists. That source is the
same great fact that the common reason of
man long ago discerned when it called our
world by that luminous name, "the universe." The great cosmic system turns on a
single axis. It forms a majestic unity. We
are all parts of an infinite organism. The
vegetable and the animal kingdom, the material
and the spiritual, each depend on one another.
Man is inseparably bound to man, as the
polyps in a polyp-colony to one another.
Even the savage knows that he is no self-
sufficient unit, but that he owes his existence
to parents who have begotten and nursed him,
and that his life is conditioned on his fellows
for its comfort or misery, for its success or
failure. And the advance of civilization and
discovery only makes this union closer, more
indispensable, more noticeable. Commerce

extends men's social ties from tribe to nation, from fellow-citizen to foreigner, from continent to continent, till the whole human race is immeshed in one close-woven net of mutual relations. And as science searches into man's history, it gives in the past an even more extensive scope to this dependence; for it shows that what we are to-day is but the accumulated activity of all our ancestors from the very beginning of life, not even omitting the monad and the monad's struggles. Evolution shows the growth of the individual to be something that all the past has contributed to, — something that is blended with all present social life, and determinative of future social welfare.

In the other parts of his philosophy Mr. Spencer has seen clearly this solidarity of the universe, and has even called his system of philosophy, in view of it, the Synthetic Philosophy. It is all the more strange that in his ethics he should have so much neglected it, for it is the very foundation of morals.

Life on earth forms one continuous whole. Human society is a great vital unity, all whose parts exist in an indispensable interdependence and interaction. No one prospers by himself alone, and no one suffers by himself alone. The interests of the individual and the interests of the community are inseparable. Egoistic pleasure, as M. Guyau well says, is "an illusion ; I can reap no pleasure separate from that of others. For all society co-works in it, from the little society that surrounds me, my family, to the great society, the community in which I live." These social relations, enveloping the highest and lowest in their intermeshed and vibrant network, form a veritable social organism with a pulsing life superior to that of any of the individuals composing its parts.

Now, it is out of this common life of the social organism that arise the common rights and duties that constitute the moral life of humanity. Our moral obligations are no illusive or merely subjective phenomena, but

a part of the very nature of things, — the necessary conditions of social health, growth, and
permanence.   As the social whole has a certain
constitution, the social parts and members
must have certain relations, in order that they
may work in a normal fashion.   It is these
relations of the members of society to one
another and to their surroundings that supply
to ethics the facts that constitute its data.
These relations are realities, — either results of
past forces that have been active, or else forces
that are still acting.   The relation, for example,
of a parent to his child, or a citizen to the state
in time of danger, is a real energy in determining the dynamic equilibrium or course of
development of the social organism.   And as
the members of society mutually lean upon
one another, and mutually interact and modify
each other's course and progress, all must move
together according to universal laws to produce
general welfare, harmony, and progress.   In
this solidarity of social life lies the real ground
and reason for Kant's formal law of ethics, —

" So will that the maxim of thy conduct may become a universal law for all moral beings." Belonging to one moral system, as all men do, no individual can ignore or rebel against the general law of the whole without injury to his neighbor, any more than one of the planets could rush from its orbit without throwing into perturbation all the rest of our solar system.

As soon as we see certain relations in existence, we see, as involved by them, certain corresponding feelings and acts, as the only ones befitting, under the circumstances. The dependence of children upon their parents, for example, demands corresponding feelings of reverence and willing obedience. The intimate union of husband and wife demands an equally intimate love and confidence. Suffering is the natural consequence of vice, happiness of conscious virtue. The worker who does much for the good of others ought to receive much; he who does little ought to receive little. He who commits evil, deserves cor-

responding retribution. If you see it to be
your right to be treated by your neighbor in
a certain manner, then it is your duty to treat
him in the same manner if the circumstances
be reversed. These laws of reciprocity and
distributive justice underlie all social activity.
A power that makes for righteousness turns
all the currents of society, in the long run, in
one direction, — the direction of truth and
right; for those acts and thoughts that are
truthful and rightful are the only ones that
are self-consistent and capable of surviving in
the struggle for existence; they are the only
ones whose ultimate result tends to minister
to the permanent enrichment and elevation
of human life. The benefits acquired by
injustice are benefits which turn into curses, —
curses which sooner or later come home to
roost and plague the inventor.

Morality is, therefore, no accidental thing,
but a necessary law. It is no artificial compact,
but the inherent principle of social relations. It
is not a result of statutes; for all statutes and

ordinances are but man's more or less bungling attempts to reproduce the moral laws which the nature of things has, from the beginning of human society, prescribed. Neither can we refer the origin and ground of right, as old-fashioned systems of ethics have done, to the divine will simply, or to the revelation of it given in the Bible or other sacred scripture. This is equally inadmissible. For on this theory, if some new revelation of the divine will be produced, if some ancient codex be unearthed in Egypt or Syria with a new reading, or some learned translator correct the old translation of a commandment, or some new prophet appear and, in the name of some miraculous cure or gift of levitation or second sight, convince men that he is a messenger from God, and by such new revelations or interpretations, that which used to be forbidden is now enjoined, or that which used to be permitted is henceforth forbidden, — in such a case, right and wrong must simultaneously change places. But before the tribunal of rational ethics such moral revolutions are inadmissible. That which is right to-day must, under similar circumstances, be right to-morrow. That which is right at all must be right in itself, not because of somebody else's word. The Jewish Decalogue and all the rest of the moral precepts of the Scriptures are but reflections of the morals of that race and time, — not originators of right and wrong. The distinction between sin and righteousness is not made by any fiat, even of the Almighty. The reason that injustice is wrong, is not because it is forbidden by divine edicts, but it is wrong whether forbidden or not, — as wrong before Moses received the ten tables as it was after it. And if supernatural authority might be supposed to command the wrong and condemn the right, the eternal laws of righteousness would not be thereby subverted, but to every genuinely moral nature this alleged supernatural authority would thereby itself be discredited and no longer be reverenced as divine.

The law of right is therefore as independent of authority, human or celestial, as it is everlasting. Can we resolve it, then, as the new ethical theorists would, into an evolution of the laws of comfort, or into elements supplied by the greatest happiness of the greatest number? Just as little. No desire or pleasure of a multitude can any more create a moral law than the desire or pleasure of one individual. If ten thousand men can secure their own happiness by wronging a single poor man, that does not make such wrong a righteous deed. The wrong still remains wrong, however many are made happy, and right is right, however many be sacrificed in its defence; for, as Wendell Phillips so nobly said, right is " that absolute essence of things which lives in the sight of the eternal and the infinite."

The moral law is seated in the very structure of the universe; for it is the natural concord which manifests the unity of being, and is as indispensable to social existence as the force of gravitation to the continuance of the planetary system. Immorality is the discord which appears when the forces of nature have ceased to co-ordinate themselves, and rushing off on their own divided, self-willed paths, terminate in some monstrous birth or despicable ruin.

CHAPTER II.

IT is thus from the fundamental *unity of life* and the normal *relations* of *men* in *society* that our duties flow; for these are the very conditions of social existence.

What, then, shall we take as our supreme moral end and regard as our chief duties?

Now, the evident end of any being is to *be*, according to the nature given to him. If the rose does not blossom, if the bee does not fly and gather honey, we say they have not fulfilled their destinies. If, then, the being be a rational and moral being, it evidently has a more elevated end, — that end which its fuller intelligence discerns and the higher constitution of its nature points to. This end is the amplest, loftiest development of which its being is capable.

When we look at the great law of evolution, we find that the most conspicuous feature in it is that it is a constantly ascending path. The direction of the process of the worlds is an upward one. It has marched steadily onward from simpler to more complex forms; from the inanimate to the animate; from the unconscious to the conscious; from the merely sentient to the rational; from the impersonal and involuntary to the personal and voluntary. This ascent of life is, by superficial thinkers, explained as a simple result of that competitive struggle for existence between lower and higher forms which Mr. Darwin calls Natural Selection and which he has so fully illustrated. But Natural Selection only explains the extinction of the lower and less well-organized species and the survival of the higher; it does not explain the origin of the higher. The only explanation which Mr. Darwin has for this is that of a tendency to variation which is constantly acting in all directions. Mr. Spencer explains it by the supposition of a natural adaptation of the vital forces to an improved environment. On either theory we have to suppose an original *expansive* power in vital forces, ready, like an elastic gas, to enter in and improve every opportunity for larger life. As M. Guyau has so acutely pointed out, biology presents to us as a fundamental law that life is not merely nutrition, but it is *fecundity* and *production* as well. It is of its very essence, as it goes on, appropriating food and assimilating it, to *enlarge* itself, to accumulate a superabundance of force, and next, to overflow and beget new life. The more it acquires, the more necessary is it that it should give forth again. Life, like fire, preserves itself only by communicating itself. The plant must grow, must bloom, must sow its seeds, or it withers away. In living beings there is always, therefore, *a pressure toward larger and higher existence.* Hence, wherever the conditions of the world allow, life takes on superior forms, equips itself with more efficient organs and faculties, ascends to higher and higher realms of life.

In that part of the evolutionary pathway

below the stage of humanity, the more noticeable thing is the increasing perfection of the
physical organism.   But even in the animal
kingdom every higher species shows an increase in the rational element, progressive
penetration and saturation of flesh by spirit,
moulding the organism more flexibly to higher
ends ; and when in man the flexile hands and
the erect attitude are reached, the climax of
bodily evolution seems to be attained, and the
material and outward progress gives place to
an inward one.   Intelligence by its control
over the forces of Nature, its previsions of
danger or advantage, its ingenious production
of instruments and discovery of creation's se-
crets, is found to be a more efficient power
than any mammoth's strength or gazelle's
swiftness or tiger's fury.   With daily exercise,
thought and love unfold in a marvellous ratio,
till the civilized man has passed farther beyond the ape than the ape beyond the worm.

The characteristic of the process of vital
evolution is thus seen to be the steady mani-

festation in matter of more and more imma-
terial energy, and the more complete outflowing
and perfection of the activity of the spirit.
As thought and love in their noble unfolding
carry man up to the heights of the spiritual
life, these higher qualities of soul are seen
to be more precious than anything that has
preceded them. They are recognized as the
only things that have worth in themselves.
Any broad and rational idea of human welfare
enlarges it to the conception of something more
than happiness. As Prof. Harold Höffding,
the distinguished Utilitarian of Denmark, has
admitted: "Welfare is an illusion if we understand by it a passive condition of things created for all. It must consist in action, work,
development. Rest can only mean a termi-
nation for the time being, the attainment of
a new level upon which it is possible for
a new course of development to proceed." So
Madame Royer, in the preface to her recent
work, has enlarged the conception of the good
to that "which increases in the world the

quantity of conscious existence." But inasmuch as pain and the desire to avoid it have probably done more to develop consciousness than pleasure has, we have here a different and much larger standard of moral good than happiness. The pessimists, such as Schopenhauer and Hartmann, would have us believe that as life evolves, pain and misery constantly increase. The optimists are just as sure that with the evolution of life, happiness increases *pari passu.* These two large schools here blankly contradict one another. But there is one point on which they agree, and this is one also that all candid observation confirms; namely, that with the progressive development of life, consciousness undergoes a corresponding development in sensitiveness, power, and elevation. The long story of evolution is the story of the steady unfolding of consciousness, from the dim stirrings of but half-awakened feeling in mollusk and radiate, up through successive ranges of thought and desire in brute and savage to the full self-knowledge and open-

eyed vision of the modern man. Our pleasures, of course, have increased, both in variety
and intensity; but so have our pains. If the
delight of the artist in his ideal creation is
something beyond that of any bird in its jocund
morning song, equally does the mother's anguish over her dead child exceed any pain that
the animal world knows. Weighed in the scales
of hedonism, life does not seem to have gained
much. But measure the amplitude and elevation of *personality*, and we see in the wider
and deeper emotions of humanity, in man's
larger faculties and activities, in his clearer
insight, his purer will, his nobler aims, his
fuller and higher life, a most wonderful gain.
The more we study the world and its constitution, the more we see that the thing which
it has at heart is to bring forth *consciousness*,
and to bring it forth in greatest fulness. This
purpose is embedded in the inmost tissues of
this organic whole which we call the universe. All the organs and instincts of man
tend to preserve and carry forward the species.

All that is about us and with which we come in contact stirs us up for the same end. Whenever desire awakens, we begin to seek after something which will be better for ourselves. And we soon see that this means not merely the attainment of more outward possessions but of a better manhood, — stronger personal powers, keener faculties, higher virtues. The animal is developed simply by external conditions and stimuli. But man is not only drifted onward by these currents of nature, he is himself the steersman of his destiny, the developer of his own being. With the capacity of recalling and reflecting on the past, and that introspection which constitutes self-consciousness, man inevitably asks himself, "Have I made the best of my opportunities? Have I made the best of myself?" And out of this sense of responsibility for becoming what I should be, there springs up next, as Professor Green points out, an ideal of character and virtue. The man conceives a possible better state of himself, and strives to make it actual. This

effort at a more full realization of his own
manhood may move upon a comparatively low
plane, in which case it manifests itself merely
as the spring of arrogance, pride, the eager
push for pleasures or honors, or other form
of sordid self-seeking and self-assertion. But
if these worldly prizes are found to be unsatis-
factory, and the mind reaches after higher and
more lasting means of realizing its capabilities,
then this impulse may become the source of
the noblest aspirations after moral and spiritual perfection. This vision of a perfect humanity will be at first, of course, only faintly
discerned. But however poor and crude the
ideal of complete manhood be, "it keeps the
man," as has well been said, "in the pathway of
human progress." And unless he strives after
this fulfilment of all that becomes a man, he
feels himself in woful debt to the Author of
his being. He has received from the creative
source this rich endowment of faculties as a
gift, and he owes to that source a correspond-

ing return. He *ought* to make such return ;
otherwise, the spectacle of this wasted life and
endowment continually confronts him with
mute reproaches for his unfaithfulness. It is
a spectacle of inconsistency and inequity that
violates the unities of the universe, instinctively rousing the mind of the spectator to
condemnation, and stinging the perpetrator to
remorse. Duty is thus seen to be the equation demanded by conscience between our
actual and our ideal manhood. "The moral
personality of humanity" ought therefore, as
Kant says, to be recognized as something that
never ought to be degraded into a means to
anything else. It is an end in itself. The
ultimate standard of worth is personal worth,
and the only progress that is worth striving
after, the only acquisition that is truly good
and enduring, is the growth of the soul, the
realization of our true and higher self, in that
fulness of powers and elevation of character
that constitute the moral perfection to which

man instinctively strives. Unless social improvement includes the improvement of the character and inner life of the individual members of the race, it is a sham and a delusion.

CHAPTER III.

THE ultimate end of a moral being is therefore the development of his spiritual personality to the fullest, noblest, and highest life possible.

But as a moral being, this prize cannot be sought or secured for himself alone. As we have seen, each individual is, to use Mr. Leslie Stephen's apt phrase, a part of the social tissue of the great organism in which he was born; and in virtue of this vital unity, his own good can be obtained only in conjunction with the good of his fellows.

Through the great laws of descent and inheritance, all the generations of life, not only from the beginning of human life, but from that of animal life, are bound together in a continuous vital chain. The whole stem and fibre of our sensitive and mental constitution are rooted in the relations that bind man to

man, and humanity to the sentient life below,
out of which it has arisen. In the light of
modern science, humanity is one vast organism,
whose span of life runs back to the very dawn
of animal existence upon the earth. We who
are now on the stage are not only the inher-
itors of the past, but the living embodiments
and trustees of the life of the future. By our
unfaithfulness and negligence we can retard
and mar the progress of humanity ; by our dili-
gence and loyalty we preserve and further it.
As the child is father to the man, as the habits,
efforts, and even ideals of the youth still live
within the statesman and the philosopher, so
the thoughts and deeds of our ancestors live
in the spiritual life of to-day, and ours shall
live in the victories or disappointments of posterity. We have no more a right than we have
a possibility of living to ourselves alone, or for
the present, independent of the past and the
future.

Any ethical system that is in harmony with
modern scientific knowledge therefore puts the

individual into universal relations with every other and the whole; it regards him as a vital part of the social organism, by whose circulating blood of common wealth and thought and good-will he is daily nourished. We are bound therefore, in our moral decisions, to recognize these universal relations of every meanest individual. We are bound to weigh our actions and motives with regard to their influence on the elevation or depression of the human race as a whole. The great law of duty is to make, not one cell or nerve of the body politic flourish, but the great all-connected whole of social life progress to higher life, rational, emotional, moral, and spiritual.

The ultimate standard, then, for determining what is morally good and morally bad is its tendency to help forward or impede this progress of our race toward the ideal of humanity. The supreme end of moral action is the evolution of the completest and highest soul-life of humanity. Those motives are morally good which aim to promote higher life in humanity, which we judge most conducive to lifting us and the race, with which we are inseparably united, toward more exalted and perfect soul-life. Those motives are morally bad which tend to lower, impede, or degrade this spiritual development. This is an end and this is a standard which is not, like that of happiness, dangerous and ineffective as an immediate aim, and to be *"entirely set aside"* as a guide "throughout a large part of conduct," as, Mr. Spencer [1] admits, must be done with that of "*happiness*," but it is one that can be directly, safely, and advantageously applied.

This is a principle of moral judgment radically different from any form of hedonism, and yet in strictest harmony with the law and principles of evolution. Indeed, it seems to me the only ethical end and standard consistent with intelligent loyalty to this great principle of modern science. Mr. Spencer himself has incidentally acknowledged this goal of " highest

[1] Data of Ethics, pp. 155, 156.

life" as "the naturally revealed end toward which the Power manifested throughout evolution works," and "recognizes it as a logical consequent" that, "conforming to those principles by which the highest life is achieved, is furthering that end."[1] And he has also admitted that "the doctrine that perfection or excellence of nature should be the object of pursuit is in one sense true; for it tacitly recognizes that ideal form of being which the highest life implies, and to which evolution tends."[2]

But, unfortunately, throughout the greater part of his treatise he drops down from this clear height into the marshland where happiness is regarded as the supreme end, and the surplus of pleasure or pain (the more or less general, indirect, and re-representative quality of the motive) becomes his ethical test and source of authority. His system of morals becomes thus confused, inconsistent, and seriously impaired; for the supreme end, "happi-

[1] Data of Ethics, p. 171.   [2] Ibid., p. 172.

ness," which he has substituted for that " highest life" toward which evolution tends, is, as
he admits himself, only "a concomitant" of
that highest life.[1] Why does he substitute this
subordinate concomitant for the grander orb
in whose train it follows? This is to put
the part for the whole. It is making the
satellite of the system the centre, and demanding that the central orb revolve around that,
and results inevitably in throwing Mr. Spencer's ethical system into the same confusion
in which our ideas of the solar system were
involved before Copernicus put the sun in the
centre where it belonged. Nay, more than this,
the seeking of happiness is not only not the
whole, nor the chief part of human life, but it
is not even the most characteristic part of our
being. The conscious seeking of pleasure is only
a consequence of the instinctive effort to maintain and increase life; and our success in
gaining pleasure is a symptom and incident
merely, and often a most irregular and dispro-

[1] Data of Ethics, p. 172.

portionate incident, of our vital health and
activity.   It is through its practical, though
crude, service as such a symptom that happiness has come to be taken as a moral guide.
But it is not only true, as Spencer admits, that
it is dangerous for the individual to make
it his immediate aim, but even to make
the happiness of the race the moral aim would
tend to deteriorate humanity.   Its influence
would be to draw mankind down toward the
animal life.   Pain has always been and will
always be, I fancy, an essential condition of
the upward movement of humanity.

Or suppose that pleasure, as often happens,
especially when very intense, becomes destructive of life.   Is it still to be taken as a
test of the moral worth of conduct?   Or
suppose a society converted to pessimism, and
that by the philosophical poison of this theory,
birth and growth and the preservation and
development of life should become sources
of sorrow to it, and decay and death should
become its themes of rejoicing and sources of

happiness. In such a society the begetting of children, as Schopenhauer and Buddhists have said, would be naturally called a sin, and suicide and murder be rated virtues. But would such antipodal moral judgments be, in such a society, correct ethics ? Are morals to be legitimately revolutionized by the adoption of such a theory ? If they may not legitimately be thus transmuted, we must recognize as the supreme end something more stable than man's idea of happiness. And this is to be found in that fulness and elevation of life of which happiness is the normal accompaniment. All noble traits of character — intelligence, power, loving-kindness, courage, resolution — are therefore natural goods, and, like beauty, carry their authority within themselves. And whatever tends to produce this higher life and more perfect character, whatever is a sure sign that it is becoming developed, ethics should regard as good.

CHAPTER IV.

IT is evident, however, with a very little reflection, that all things are not equally conducive to this development of the perfect life. In the animal kingdom, for example, different creatures vary in what they contribute toward bringing the whole of being toward perfection. Those which contribute little are to be restrained or ignored; those whose influence is for the most part antagonistic to this end, are to be suppressed. Hence, beasts of prey and insect pests and other enemies of our race are rightly to be swept out of the ascending path of life. In the human kingdom, again, we find a hierarchy of moral values and corresponding rights. There are parts of it which are inferior, subordinate means and instruments; and there are other parts which are superior, because nearer to the great end of our being. Each part has its rights, even the most animal passion, just as every animal species has its rights. But the lower must keep to their subordinate place, and not encroach upon the higher. On the contrary, when there comes a conflict and one must be given up, — thought or the pleasures of the table ; liberty or low comfort ; maternal love or self-indulgence ; honesty or a good bargain, — then morality calls upon us to sacrifice the lower and preserve the higher. The rule is to be found in conformity to that which conduces to the evolution of the completest and highest soul life ; and there is consequently a gradation of moral values corresponding to the varying levels of the evolution of humanity. Moreover, as the level of civilization, and especially the ideal of a true human life, rises, that which was at one time a virtue, because relatively an advance, now becomes a vice, because relatively a retardation, of human progress, a bar to the upward march of our soul-life.

CHAPTER V.

A S the standard of morality is, then, this ideal of human perfection, it is evident, in the next place, that morality is essentially, as Dr. Martineau has so well insisted, a preferential choice between higher and lower alternatives. "As the instinctive impulses turn up within us, one after another, and two or more come into the presence of each other, they report us their relative worth, and we intuitively know the better from the worse." The proper field of ethics is internal. The essence of a moral act does not lie in its result, but in the motive from which it springs. It should have its source, not in fear or self-interest, but in a reverence for the higher life and a voluntary choice of that which promotes it. It belongs properly, as we have already noticed, to persons, not to things. It does not concern itself about conduct, but only about character.

The questions on which the members of the Utilitarian school spend their time, as to the particular deeds or kind of behavior that is to be enjoined, are questions not properly and directly moral, but only indirectly so. They are questions about the wisest means or methods of embodying morality in the world around us. They belong to that second stage in which the moral artist considers through what material or in what form and color he may most prudently and wisely realize his ideal. As, at a cry of pain, the lower impulses of vexation at the irritating sound and aversion for the distressing sight contend within the man with the higher impulses of pity and sympathy, and the higher, if he be sufficiently developed, win the day, — there comes next the question how best to show this pity and realize this fellow-feeling. And in this second stage the estimation of the greater or less utility of various means, and the greater or less relief from pain or positive pleasure which they may produce, rightly comes to the front.

Yet even here the question of the useful is always to be considered in the light of that which is the supreme good, — the production of higher life, and the perfection of our mental and spiritual being.

CHAPTER VI.

ACCORDING to the usual representation of evolutionary ethics, it is only the selfish motives that are natural to man. Morality is generally considered by evolutionists as undeveloped in primitive man. The relentless struggle for existence and the inescapable doom of the vanquished in that struggle is the last word of modern biology. "The earliest instincts of primitive man," says a prominent American disciple of Mr. Spencer, in his exposition of evolution, "were doubtless purely egoistic, like that of the brutes."[1] Mr. Edward Clodd in his "Story of Creation: a Plain Account of Evolution," tells us that " man's normal state is one of conflict." So, with still stronger emphasis, Professor Huxley declares that "among animals

[1] L. G. Janes, Evolution · Popular Lectures before the Brooklyn Ethical Society, p. 262.

15

as among primitive men, the weakest and stupidest went to the wall, while the toughest and shrewdest, those who were best fitted to cope with their circumstances, but not the best in another way, survived. Life was a continuous free fight, and beyond the limited and temporary relations of the family, the Hobbesian war of each against all was the normal state of existence."[1]

How, then, does disinterestedness develop out of this primitive selfishness, and love grow out of this antagonism ? How, out of such predispositions and antecedents, has duty come to be evolved ? Is there any other explanation of these things to be found than in some such theory as Mr. Spencer has presented of the transformation of experiences of egoistic utility into faculties of moral intution, by the means of the social environment of man and the influences of heredity ?

I believe there is. The altruistic motive is as natural and primitive as the egoistic.

[1] Nineteenth Century Review, February, 1888, p. 165.

Individual altruism is no late result of the social organization of mankind, whether military, industrial, political, or ecclesiastical, but the dynamic cause lying at the root of that organization.

Peaceful and well-ordered society does not have to wait for the later man, nor even the first man, before it could come into existence. It existed ages before man, and in ranks of life far below the scale of humanity. Among the bees, the ants, the beavers, it exists in forms so highly developed as to excite the astonishment of all who have studied it. And these are not exceptional cases, except in the higher range to which the common phenomena attain. Among most birds, fishes, and herbivorous mammals the same gregarious instincts and habits prevail, in greater or less degree. No living animal exists alone; it cannot continue its species without entering into the most intimate union with some other individual of its species, and many of the lower species, like the polyp colonies, pass their existence in the most complete dependence one upon another. As Espinas, the distinguished author of "Des Sociétés animales," well says: " Life in common is no accidental fact in the animal kingdom. It does not appear here and there in a fortuitous and capricious manner. It is not the privilege of certain isolated species. It is, on the contrary, and we believe ourselves prepared to prove it abundantly in the present work, a fact normal, constant, and universal. From the lowest grades of the series to the most elevated, all animals find themselves at some moment of their existence engaged in society. The social environment is the necessary condition of the renewal and conservation of life." [1]

And as peaceful and well-organized society did not begin with man, neither altruism nor the moral instincts had their first beginning with man. It may be, as is charged, that no creature, however high in the scale of being, is absolutely unselfish. But even if this be

---

[1] Des Sociétés animales, p. 9.

true, it is equally true that hardly any man or animal, however low, is absolutely selfish. As Professor Huxley himself has, in another place, acknowledged, "Even the highest faculties of feeling and intellect begin to germinate in lower forms of life." In most warm-blooded species of animals (certainly in all the numerous species that suckle their young) the care of the mother for its progeny is essential to the survival of that progeny. And in many species, even among birds and fish, the male as well as the female parents are active in guarding the nest and feeding the young and driving away enemies. When a huntsman suddenly comes upon a brood of young pheasants, the mother-bird bravely exposes herself to the attack, and even appears to court it, to distract attention from her young; and females of species that, when not with young, seek safety at once in flight, when in charge of young heroically turn to face the enemy.

And it is not only within the narrow bounds of the family that this instinctive altruism is

found, binding the animals together and preserving them against their enemies. Wherever
animals live in social groups, they are found ex-
tending mutual aid to one another. The same
sympathetic instinct that draws them together
and gives them delight in one another's presence must lead them to give aid to each other
wherever the intelligence is developed sufficiently to see what a comrade needs or what
the band to which they belong needs. Sir
John Lubbock in his work on Ants, and Professor Romanes in his able volume on Animal
Intelligence, have given many most interesting
instances of such co-operation. In the ant's
nest the building of the house, the importation
of the food, the rearing of the progeny, and the
care of the aphides who serve as their milch
cows, are all carried on co-operatively. According to Forel, the fundamental feature in
the life of many species of ants is the fact and
the obligation of every ant to share its food,
already swallowed and digested, with every
member of the community who may apply for

it. If an ant which has its crop full is too
selfish to regurgitate a part of it for the use
of a hungry comrade, it will be treated as an
enemy, or worse. The agricultural ants of
Texas sow crops, and harvest and store them
in granaries, to use in common for mutual
sustenance. The burying beetles combine their
efforts to cover up in the ground the corpses
of mice or birds, in which to deposit their eggs.
Crabs have been seen to work for hours to turn
over into his natural position a comrade that
had been accidentally thrown on his back. The
house-sparrow faithfully informs his comrades
where grain is to be found ; and the lapwing
was well called by the Greeks the *good-mother*,
because of its habit of protecting other aquatic
birds from the attacks of their enemies. So
the meadow wag-tails, small as they are, by
calling out all their forces from over a wide
range of territory, whenever a bird of prey like
a kite or a hawk appears among them, drive
the more powerful bird away empty-handed.
Parrots not only give mutual aid to one an-

other in hunting, posting sentries, and so on,
but the attachment of two domesticated parrots
to one another has been known to be so great
that after the death of one by accident or
disease, the other has pined away and died
from grief. But especially among our simian
relatives are these customs of social life and
mutual aid almost universal. They hunt in
bands, even crossing streams on the bridges
made of their intertwined bodies ; and when
one of them, attacked by some enemy, utters
a cry of distress, the whole band rallies to the
rescue and boldly repulses the attacks of most
beasts of prey. Several species show the greatest sympathy and care for their wounded ; and
it is Darwin himself who has made known to
the world those affecting instances of animal
heroism recorded by Brehm. Especially noticeable is the story of the baboons attacked
by the dogs and successfully retreating, the
younger guarded by the older and stronger. As
they moved away, a young one, only six months
old, became detached and surrounded by the

dogs and cried for aid ; when one of the largest males came down again from the mountain, pushed through the dogs, and triumphantly led the young baboon away. The devotion and self-sacrifice of the dog for his master or drowning children is classical; and equally many and notable stories are told of their compassion for abandoned puppies, sick comrades, and even starving kittens. A wounded badger has been known to be carried away by another badger who suddenly appeared on the scene. Rats have been seen feeding a blind couple, and leading the sightless by a straw.[1] J. C. Wood tells of a weasel which came to pick up and carry away an injured comrade. Darwin tells of sightless crows that have been fed and kept alive by their more fortunate comrades; and what is more astonishing still, a blind pelican was seen by Captain Stansbury, which was fed, and well fed, by other pelicans on fish brought from a distance of thirty miles.[2]

[1] Seelenleben der Thiere, p. 64.

[2] Darwin, Descent of Man, ch. iv.

Among men we should call such actions altruistic, — nay, moral. Must we rate them as merely egoistic and unconscious because occurring among animals? Agassiz did not hesitate to call similar phenomena moral. "Who can see," he well asked, "the sunfish balancing itself over its eggs, and protecting them for weeks, without being convinced that the sentiment that guides it in these acts is the same as that which attaches the mother to her child? The gradation of moral faculties in the superior animals and in man shades so imperceptibly from stage to stage that to deny to the first a certain sense of responsibility and conscience, it would be necessary to exaggerate beyond due measure the difference which exists between them and man." [1]

Now, if altruism and a rudimentary morality, at least, appear so incontrovertibly among the superior animals, in stages of evolution far below man, is it credible that in man it should never have appeared until long after

[1] Species, p. 90.

his development to the properly human rank? I cannot believe it. It is certainly contradictory to the theory of his evolution from simian ancestors, inasmuch as the apes are notably social, and already not without altruistic predispositions.

Moreover, we may notice that this primitive altruistic instinct has been much more the true condition of success in the struggle for existence than that self-seeking of competing individuals, thirsting for one another's blood, which has been usually presented as the chief feature in evolution. In comparison with the multitudinous numbers of the social animals in nature, its flocks of migratory birds, its shoals of herring and bands of seal, its herds of reindeer, bison, wild horses, and sheep, its great families of prairie-dogs, monkeys, elephants, antelopes, and beavers, who all afford mutual aid to one another, the number of the carnivoræ or solitary and selfish animals is relatively very small. These latter are the exceptional, not the normal types of life. And the

great reason for it is that it is precisely this
social life and the altruistic instincts that .ac-
company it that afford the greatest advantage
in the competition between different tribes and
species.   Social life furnishes protection against
beasts of prey; by migrations to new homes,
impossible for single individuals to accomplish
with safety, it saves from starvation; it tides
the feeble over periods of weakness; and it
enables the species to rear progeny and keep
up their numbers, in spite of a slow birth-rate;
and above all, through daily intercourse it
stimulates the growth of intelligence as nothing else does.   Species that turn to solitary
life, and become depredators and enemies of
their fellows, in spite of their strength, swiftness, and terrible weapons, soon fall behind
in the race of life and begin to die out, as all
the carnivoræ are doing.   "Those animals,"
as Prince Kropotkin well says,[1] " which know
best how to combine, have the greatest chance
of survival and farther evolution, although they

[1] Nineteenth Century Review, November, 1890.

may be inferior to others in each of the faculties enumerated by Darwin and Wallace, save
the intellectual faculty. The highest verte-
brates, and especially mankind, are the best
proof of this assertion. As to the intellectual
faculty, while every Darwinist will agree with
Darwin that it is the most powerful arm in
the struggle for life and the most powerful
factor for further evolution, he also will admit
that intelligence is an eminently social faculty.
Language, imitation, and accumulated experience are so many elements of growing
intelligence of which the unsociable animal
is deprived."

Social co-operation, not individual self-seeking, appears thus as the chief factor of evolution. And this social life is itself conditioned
upon the instinctive altruism, the rudimentary moral sense, of the species. Unless there
is a sympathy between the different members
of a group of birds that prompts them to risk
their own safety in helping to drive off the
hawk that seizes on a comrade ; unless there is

an incipient sense of justice that leads them
to respect as his the tid-bit which a neighbor
has found, or to chastise together the member
who has appropriated the nest of a fellow, —
the social group would very quickly fall to
pieces. All naturalists who have studied
gregarious species have noticed among them
a sense of personal rights and of the duty of
just dealing with their fellow-members in the
group, as more or less developed. The dogs
in Constantinople, it is said, have each their
special street or alley to which they claim a
vested right. "Whatever the distance from
which the swallows or the crows have come,
each one returns to the nest it has built or
repaired last year." In the villages of the
prairie-dogs and beavers, each has his own
resting-place, which his comrades respect. "If
a lazy sparrow," says Prince Kropotkin, "in-
tends appropriating the nest which a comrade
is building, or even steals from it a few sprays
of straw, the group interferes against the lazy
comrade; and it is evident that without such

mutual respect for each other's haunts being the rule, no nesting association of birds could exist."

Even in the animal kingdom, then, the moral disposition exists, in either a rudimentary or fairly developed form; and its existence is the condition of the continuance of social life and the upward evolution of the species. And when we reach the human sphere, that which specially characterizes its progress is the greater and greater restriction of selfish and immoral competition by the growing sense of justice and sympathy in the community. As human society develops, it becomes daily more and more evident that the qualities that make a tribe the fittest to survive are not merely strength of body or cunning of mind, but that a trustworthy, sober, and kindly moral nature is an equal if not greater requisite. Which are the more likely to survive and rear offspring, — the peaceable, or the quarrelsome? The temperate or the intemperate? The licentious, or those among whom conjugal faithfulness and parental solicitude reign? Can any one doubt? Does not every physician know all too well how surely Nature stamps out licentiousness and intoxication by weakness of body, weakness of mind, insanity, idiocy, or childlessness, so that the continuance of the worst forms of vice in any single family or ancestral line is self-limited to a very few generations? Or take a tribe where robbery, murder, cannibalism, or infanticide prevails. Is it not plain of itself, and likewise supported by the reports of travellers, that such tribes are decaying tribes, yearly diminishing, on whose heads Nature has already pronounced sentence? Or even take such minor moral faults as laziness, cowardice, gross selfishness, lack of truthfulness and patriotism. While peace, fertility, and favoring natural conditions exist, such a community may keep its head above water; but when the crisis of war or pestilence or scant harvests come, such communities are sure to sink and perish before the competition of more sound and virtuous body politics. When from the low state of morals among certain Australians and African savages it is argued that we are given by them the proof and illustration of the general absence of moral qualities in primitive humanity, the real sequence of cause and effect has been reversed. It is, on the contrary, precisely because such tribes have been deficient in average moral quality that they have failed to march upward on the road of civilization with the rest of mankind and have fallen into these bog-holes of savage degradation. It is only when humanity is spurred by conscience to the discharge of grand duties that our race develops to the full stature of its manhood.

It is evident how much farther back we must go than to the effects of certain political and military drillings or ecclesiastical pressures before we come to the source of our moral intuitions. The sense of duty and the impulses of altruism are far older than church or monarchy, ancestor-worship or the earliest

epoch of self-conscious calculation of the
respective returns in surplus of pleasure to be
gained from immediate or future, temporary
or stable, gratifications. These feelings of
benevolence and these perceptions of sacred
obligation are instinctive from the beginning, —
inheritances from our earliest ancestors, up-
risings into consciousness and activity of the
stable laws and primeval orderliness of Nature
itself. The moral necessity that man feels is
but the full-blown blossom of that sacred unity
and natural bond that holds the ocean in its
bed and swings the planets in punctual
rhythm around their suns. The impulse to
reach out in sympathy to our fellows and to
help the needy, to regard nothing that is human
as alien to us and our duty, is an impulse as
natural as the scattering of its winged seeds
abroad upon the earth by dandelion or snap-
dragon. In the lowest orders of animated
creatures there is an expansive tendency, a
constant overflowing of the fountain of being,
commingling the waters of life and pressing

animated existence into the channels of a larger life than that of individual selfishness.

That very law of vital fecundity which directs life constantly upward, directs it also outward beyond the bounds of self. The more a living thing gains, the more (as M. Guyau has well pointed out) it must expend. As surely as exhalation accompanies inhalation, so aspiration and generosity follow acquisition in the rhythmic life of a healthy humanity. Altruistic giving is the indispensable correlative of that over-production which characterizes life wherever it is at its best. A certain disinterestedness and outgoing of sympathy and largess is as necessary to true human existence as it is for the mother of a new-born child to give her milk to the babe.

"Even in the life of the blind cell there is a principle of expansion, the result of which is that no individual can restrict himself to his own interests. The richest life finds itself also that which most tends to lavish itself, to sacrifice itself, in a certain measure to share

itself with others. Hence it follows that the
most perfect organism is also the most sociable,
and that the ideal of the individual life embraces life in common. Through this law, consequently, we find replaced at the very bases
of existence the copious source of all those
sympathetic and social instincts which the
English school has too often presented as
things acquired, more or less artificially, in the
course of evolution, therefore as more or less
adventitious." [1]   That transition from egoism
to altruism for which in hedonistic systems it
is so hard to find any justification, is therefore of the *very essence* of a soundly based system of ethics.

[1] Morale sans Obligation ni Sanction, par M. Guyau,
p. 25.

CHAPTER VII.

A ND this brings us directly to consider that critical question in ethics, What faculty of human nature is most directly concerned in moral development? In Mr. Spencer's treatise there is a capital mistake and omission, which has been greatly responsible for the artificial character which he gives to our sense of obligation and to the altruistic virtues. This is the neglect of the intellectual factor as a law-giving power and most persuasive teacher of equity. In his ethical investigations Mr. Spencer has given his attention too exclusively to the sensory and emotional side of human nature. In the Spencerian ethics man is essentially a sensitive being, not a thinking being. His character is a pure result of sense impressions either in an original or a metamorphic state. Reason is only an instrument to associate and compare the past sensations, and for the future to direct man to agreeable sensations or to warn him away from disagreeable ones. Reason is a result and transformation of sensation, but not a spontaneous or productive force. Starting from such a view of human nature, it is only a logical consequent to find the system of ethics that Mr. Spencer presents to us to be a system that takes pleasure and pain for its guides, and happiness for its ultimate end. Man naturally appears as essentially an egoist, his eye glued on his personal enjoyment; and it becomes a very delicate problem how to account for the growth of disinterestedness in humanity, and especially to find any proper sanction for that sacrifice of the personal interest to the general interest that morality has always demanded.

Mr. Spencer has committed here two serious errors, — first, in placing the root of ethics in the selfish rather than in the unselfish constituents of human nature ; second, in placing it in the realm of feeling rather than in that of reason.

Force and fear and custom may compel the person who is considering what it is most prudent for him to do to adopt a certain course of conduct. But while it is weighed in the scales of expediency, it never becomes a moral phenomenon, nor can it be transformed into a moral phenomenon till it is taken out of those scales and put into that quite other balance, whose counters are equity and duty. Sympathy is a great help in the work of lifting up our low selfishness into the loftier and diviner ether of a true disinterestedness ; but it will only carry us a small part of that distance which is necessary to give due account of the radical change involved in the passage from egoism to altruism. It will account for our readiness to relieve the pain of a friend, but not for our refraining from robbing a rich stranger or from hesitating to remove from life an enemy or hated rival. The influence of parental affection and family pride, making us

feel tenderly for children or kindred as exten-
sions of our own selfhood, to which they in a
sense belong, will spread out the realm of egoism over a very wide field.   But there is as yet
no real transition from egoism to altruism.
By the amalgam of heredity, and by the instrumentality of tribal competition destroying
those tribes among whom the interests of the
community or the social habits and instincts
had not become a second nature, even this
chasm perhaps may be bridged.   But there
still remains a large province of ethics which
even such explanations fail to account for.
There remains the idea of justice as obliga-
tory between men of different tribes or nation-
alities; the sense of honor in dealing with the
foreigner and the stranger; the outspreading
of the feelings of benevolence and righteous
obligation to all human beings, foreigners as
well as fellow-citizens.   These are not to be
accounted for by the influences of heredity and
natural selection.   For these laws come into
play only where there is competition between

different clans, tribes, nations, or social groups, struggling for the means of subsistence and development. The sympathy that aids the hungry foreigner; the sentiment that breathes in the famous line of Terence, " I regard nothing that is human as alien to me; " or the enthusiasm of humanity which animated the early Christians, — all these must have had their origin in other sources. As Mr. Sorley has well said, " No aspect of the theory of evolution seems able to account for an extension of the feeling of universal benevolence among different people or throughout different societies. This feeling has neither tended to promote the welfare of the race animated by it, to the exclusion of other competing races (for there are no competing races whom it could affect), nor can it be shown that it makes the individuals possessing it fitter to wage successful war against opposing forces than other individuals." [1]

As long as the moralist begins, then, by

[1] Ethics of Naturalism, p. 123.

considering man simply as a sensitive being,
there will always be a broad gap somewhere
between the primitive egoism that reigns
universally, and the altruism, embracing all
men in its universal sweep, that is to be
accounted for at the end of our evolution of
ethics. To free the process of development
from a most illogical break, we must begin
with a broader basis than Mr. Spencer does.
We must recognize that it is not chiefly
because man is a *feeling* being that he is a
moral agent, but rather because he is a *thinking*
being. The creature who cannot think may
have certain altruistic instincts, as even the
mother-bear and the brooding eagle have when
their progeny or nest are attacked. But
such feelings alone can carry their possessor
but a little way forward on the road of morality. The chief source of ethics is in *thought*,
— in the action of the reason upon our relations to others. Its essential root is in what
Fouillée so well calls the *impersonality* of
the reason. Feeling is essentially subjective ;

its tendency is therefore to overrate the importance of the self. The little pain in my own body counts a hundred times as much as a great pain in my neighbor's body, and the obtaining of a dinner or other small pleasure for myself is pursued with much more earnestness than the winning of some far greater prize to be enjoyed by my companion. Every one knows with what calm philosophy a friend's disappointments are borne, however great; and what tears, what objurgations, on the contrary, the upsetting of the broiled chicken for which your mouth is already watering, or the breaking of your favorite piece of china by an awkward servant, will give rise to. It is this essential partiality of feeling that has always been a stumbling-block in any pathway by which utilitarianism has sought to attain any sanction for the higher virtues or any rule for righteous conduct consistent with its theory. For its great commandment, "Seek the greatest happiness of the greatest number," rests upon the previous assumption that "Every one should count for one, and no one for more than one." For it is only on the supposed equality in value of one person's happiness, whoever he be, with every other, that the happiness of the greater number should overweigh the happiness of a smaller number. But on the principle of *sensibility* and the comparative weight of pleasures, there is no basis for this; for in the ever unequally loaded scales of feeling, a very small twinge in Number One's eyetooth will overweigh intensest suffering in the person of half a dozen strangers. It is the development and exercise of the intellectual faculty that raises conduct out of this slough of selfishness and partiality, and carries it to the higher fields of altruism. The social impulses naturally begin the work, and bring the human race together, just as they bring the higher order of animals together. The inherent laws of social relations are not at first perceived, but by the competition of tribes and families they are to a certain extent unconsciously worked out. Those which act out of harmony with them go to the wall, and those societies in which there is not the necessary amount of rudimentary morality to cement them, go to pieces. But when reason is unfolded, as in man, these laws that determine the fitting and consistent relations between social beings disclose themselves to the mind and conscience. The few simple principles of higher motive, that love is better than hate, that honesty is more fitting than deceit, that what we demand from others we should be ready to give to others under similar circumstances, are directly perceived and become moral intuitions, marking out the path of duty.

In the first place, the growth of reason teaches us that the misfortunes that have overcome a comrade may, under similar circumstances, overtake ourselves, and make us likewise need assistance, and thus our instinctive sympathy is reinforced by the powerful alliance of rational prudence and wise forecast. In the next place, the reason, as we have already hinted, is marked by a peculiar character of impersonality. While feeling is essentially subjective, reason is as essentially objective. It has a natural tendency to the impersonal and the universal. To make use again of some of M. Fouillée's clear statements, " It is of the very nature of thought to go out toward *others.* It is a philosophic axiom that any clear idea of the *me* involves with it as correlative an idea of a *not-me,* something other than .self. As soon as I use my reason about my *self*, I make an abstraction of this self and its personal sensibility. It is recognized as one among a thousand other selves of the same general character, and there is seen to be no objective reason why the happiness of this self of mine should be preferred above the happiness of any of these other selves. And if there are subjective reasons, — reasons due to my peculiar personal relation to this happiness, — it is recognized to be the very task of reason to elevate a man above these warping influences of egoistic incli-

nation, and to look upon his own happiness
as nearly as possible as an impartial spectator
would. Now if, in looking at myself as an
impartial spectator, I see that I need happiness, that my nature without it is like a
broken column, and unsatisfied in its tendency
toward the complete and universal, reason
affirms that my fellow-men about me, of whom
I am but a single example, also need and
ought to have happiness." It is reason, then,
pre-eminently that justifies the claim that each
human life, to be a reasonable life, should have
its share of happiness, and that in determining
what is for the good of the community " each
one should count for one, and no one for more
than one." The partial feeling may never
recognize this ; but before the cool, observing
eye of reason, this maxim is just as self-evident
as that one is less than two. From this simple
axiom of " *the moral equality of personalities*,"
distributive justice is quickly deduced, egoism
flowers into a rational altruism, and the vin-
dication of rights grows into the obligation of

duties. Even in the family, even among the animals, we see this rule of reason initiating the reign of justice. In the field of competitive struggle each gets what his superior strength or skill can seize and hold; but wherever a parent provides for the wants of a young family, there the food is distributed on another principle, — the principle of equal division to equal needs. The mother-bird gives each its due share in its respective turn. When the family swells to the clan, and the patriarch or chieftain divides the booty gained in some foray, or the products produced by some common work, the same simple rules of distribution, where one mouth counts but one in the division of food, however strong the warrior may be, again prevails. In primitive life there must have been even more frequent occasions for such division than with us, for a large part of their enterprises must have been those where only the co-operative exertions of a considerable band could bring success; and this equal distribution of the results of the common labor (except, of course, a special share to the chieftain) would be the obvious and only satisfactory method of division, wherever reason is even moderately developed.

17

CHAPTER VIII.

THAT the moral nature of man has been developed from very crude beginnings, I do not dispute; but I contend that it has not been manufactured out of purely unmoral or sensational elements, but has grown from a genuinely moral germ. If no creative fiat can be believed to create something out of nothing, still less is evolution able to perform such a contradiction. It is not strange that travellers who are destitute of philosophical training, and who behold among the savages whom they visit most revolting customs, should pronounce the moral sense completely wanting in them; and it is not strange that evolutionist philosophers, who naturally desire to start the process of development with the smallest possible capital, should exult in such statements, and should essay to build up the moral faculties and ideas from the lower

·

ground of sensation and utility. But the moral fruits that humanity produces require a moral potentiality to start with. Even on the theory of evolution, the moral germ must have been in existence previous to man. For if the moral sense in man, like other faculties, has been developed by natural selection, choosing, preserving, and unfolding the good, then the good (as that stalwart utilitarian and evolutionist, Professor Gizycki, admits) must have been already there to have been thus chosen and unfolded.[1] Otherwise there would have been no subject for natural selection to act on. The accumulation and preservation of the first moral habits could only have occurred on the condition that they satisfied the needs of a pre-existing moral sense. Many of the very darkest facts which the traveller in savage lands sets forth logically postulate a rudimentary sense of right and wrong as existing in the very lowest tribes,— an embryonic conscience which under favorable

[1] Manual of Ethical Philosophy, p. 293.

circumstances will grow into a well-developed conscience.

This moral germ, of course, does not include much love of the neighbor, or consciousness of obligation to him. It starts with only a dim, fierce sense of personal rights, manifested by instincts of self-defence and resistance to trespassers. The most careful observers of the social life of savages clearly discern these incipient moral traits. Mr. Staniland Wake, for example, in his "Evolution of Morality," after an exhaustive examination of uncultivated peoples generally, both in the Old World and the New, concludes that there is one element invariably present, — a sense of right. "It manifests itself first as a sense of right to life, and afterward, or it may be contemporaneously, as a sense of right to personal property. That the savage feels his right to life is shown by the passion with which he defends it, — a passion into which he breathes a quasi-moral indignation against attacks which he is conscious are wrongs attempted to be done to him." In the same way he equally feels a right to personal property, to the game he has caught, the produce of the ground which he has cultivated, the skins of the animals with which he clothes himself, and the hut he builds, or the cave he has excavated or used as his home. This sense of personal right to life and property doubtless goes back to the very beginning of man's career as man. For even in his simian cousins, and in animals far lower in the scale, it already plainly exists. The higher birds evidently feel a rightful claim to their nests, which they manifest by the indignation with which they repel any invasion of it. So the wild beasts feel a right to their dens, and the hen to the worm it has disinterred. The dog has a still fuller and more abiding sense of property; for he not only claims his bone as his own while he is devouring it, but he buries it for future enjoyment, and resists as an infringement on his proprietary claims any intermeddling with his hoarded tid-bits. And not only do animals exhibit their sense of vested

right in such things by the extraordinary
energy, the indignant fury, we may say, with
which they defend their claims, but they are
also often seen to respect these rights in other
animals. For a beaver, or prairie-dog, or one
of the social nesting-birds to usurp a comrade's nest is the exception, not the rule;
and in not a few species, such acts of usurpa-
tion are punished, not merely by the one dis-
possessed, but by his comrades, who unite with
him to chastise and drive away the lawless
encroacher. Thus, out of the instinct of self-
possession grows the instinct of property and
the sense of personal rights, leading the lowest
savage to repel encroachments upon his accus-
tomed sphere of life and use; for in the life
of the savage, all the simple property which
he has — food, weapons, cave or hut — is directly connected with his personal life. The
instinct of self-preservation, therefore, as Staniland Wake says,[1] directly leads to that of
property and to the sense of right which is

[1] Evolution of Morality, i. 302.

associated with it. It is exactly the same instinct which, as we have already seen, leads an animal to defend the food it has obtained, or the habitation it has formed.

CHAPTER IX.

NOW, how can we make the transition from this sense of personal right to the sense of duty, from the claim of justice for one's self to the felt obligation to give it to others? Mr. Spencer, determined to walk only in the boggy path of sensationalism, has to resort to awkward and complicated explanations, derived from the working of hereditary habits, inherited fears, and sympathetic devotion mechanically produced by the pressure of society. Not only is this clearly seen in his account of the origin of the sense of duty in the "Data of Ethics," but in his more recent and enlarged expositions of justice given in the "Nineteenth Century Review" for April, 1890, p. 612, he maintains that "the altruistic sentiment of justice can come into existence only by the aid of a sentiment which temporarily supplies its place and restrains the actions prompted by pure egoism." "This pro-altruistic sentiment," as he calls it, "which contains none of the altruistic sentiment of justice," but serves temporarily to cause respect for one another's claims, is made up, he believes, of the following components: "the dread of retaliation, the dread of social dislike, the dread of legal punishment, and the dread of the vengeance of the ancestral ghost and divine punishment. Through these restraints, the primitive tendency to pursue the objects of desire without regard to the interests of fellow-men is checked, and social co-operation made possible."

Now, very likely these external restraints have a certain measure of indirect influence in supplying favorable conditions for the growth of altruistic justice. But they are not of themselves sufficient. The chief and vital cause is not found among them. "This soft-solder of egoism and sensibilities," as Fouillée well calls it, "by which the individual is sought to be transformed into an altruist," is no doubt quite ingenious; but with equal cer-

tainty it may be pronounced a very cumbrous
expedient, and one not at all satisfactory, as
I have already pointed out, to a mind that asks
a sufficient reason for the transformation.

The idea of right is quite definitely formed,
and quite actively in operation, in periods and
stages of development long anterior to that
social organization when legal punishments
or the dread of ghostly vengeance or divine
retribution, or the other pro-altruistic restraints
which Mr. Spencer supposes, come into play.
And if this idea of right did not already exist,
none of the legal or social penalties would do
more than add to the expediency of the action.
They would not supply that peculiar undecomposable element of *rightness* which characterizes the ethical feeling.   The fear of retribution
from the spirit of the dead and the dread of
divine punishment, which Mr. Spencer would
employ as one of the powerful developing
influences in producing the moral sense, may
more reasonably be considered as themselves
among the most striking manifestations of that

moral sense. They are but crude and super-stitious forms of that remorse which, most forcibly of all, witnesses to the power of con-science. Moreover, the superstitious regard for the spirits of the dead, and dread of their pun-ishment upon the living in case certain things are done or not done, is not a thing founded merely on fear of retribution, but is also, as Mr. Wake has shown, founded largely on a pre-existing recognition of supposed rights of the departed spirit to certain obsequies, offerings, or vengeance upon his enemies. The expecta-tion that the spirit of the unburied will afflict his relatives is based on the underlying idea that the spirit has certain rights of burial and funeral service, and that it is a duty of his descendants to discharge these obligations.

Mr. Spencer's explanations of the sense of duty are too far-fetched. More simple and direct explanations are easily to be found. As adjacent hills imply a valley between them, as the birth of a child logically presup-poses the existence of parents, so the existence

of rights logically postulates that of duties.
The natural corollary of my own right is a
corresponding duty in myself to maintain that
right, and a duty in my neighbor to respect
it. When one sees a thing to be right and
good, it is the most natural of impulses to do
it. If the right is strongly felt, the sense of
obligation to do that right becomes a veritable
internal pressure, an instinctive command and
self-constraint which springs up simultaneously
with the recognition of the right.

Duty is thus logical consistency in conduct;
the equation between our social demands and
our personal deeds; the dues which the individual owes to the body politic and its various
members to square his account. This ethical
self-consistency at first only recognizes and
manifests the duty which we owe to ourselves
and our own claims, giving them their imperative urgency and special sanction. But even
in this primitive sphere it spreads far beyond
the boundaries and force of self-interest, and
urges the man to maintain his proper claims

in spite of all the dictates of prudence. The injured or menaced man maintains his rights not merely as far as calculation and expediency advise, but in indignant scorn of consequences. As reason develops so as to form general notions of man as man, of right as right, the result is that the sense of right belonging to one's self would be extended to the man's family, and next to the tribe; and as social intercourse became more intimate, the interests of all the members would be seen to be common interests, and the sense of personal rights would be extended to all members of the fraternity of the tribes. The encroachment against self which was regarded as a wrong would, by the power of mental generalization, be recognized as equally wrong when directed against a fellow-tribesman. Our neighbors and fellow-tribesmen would be seen to have rights which the assault of a foreigner interfered with, and also to have rights which ought to be sacred, even against the attack of a fellow-tribesman; and thus it would soon be seen that it was the duty of the community to protect the rights of all who belonged to it against their enemies, both external and internal. And next, it would be seen that to be consistent, we should respect those rights against ourselves ; and in obedience to the duty which we owe to others we should restrain our own most urgent desires. No doubt, experience and opportunity have their subordinate *rôle* to play in bringing the sense of duty, implicitly comprehended in our sense of right, into a conscious apprehension of obligation ; but it is chiefly due to the increased clearness and breadth of the mental vision itself. As reason develops and the selfish sensibility loses its predominance, man becomes able to look at things from an impersonal standpoint. The sense of right stretches beyond the subjective sphere and becomes objective. Reciprocity becomes almost an intuitive law of social intercourse. The claim of rights for one's self are seen to have, as necessary correlates, a recognition of corresponding duties

to those around us. The rule for to-day, it is
seen, must be acknowledged as the rule for
to-morrow also. The rule for our right conduct toward others must, in the same circumstances, be the same as the rule we have or
would set up for their right conduct toward
us. Prof. C. C. Everett, in a very suggestive
paper upon the ultimate facts of ethics, published in the "Unitarian Review" for Decem-
ber, 1887, has well pointed out that while
certain of the moral elements, such as love,
piety, and self-sacrifice, may be derived from
the altruistic instincts, such as the instinct of
sympathy, there are other equally prominent
and distinctive ethical elements, such as truthfulness, justice, honesty, and purity, which
cannot be accounted for in this way. The
source of these Professor Everett would find in
the sense of honor, and this sense he would
trace further back, — to the instinct of self-
assertion. Much ingenuity is shown in thus
deriving the various virtues from personal,
family, or natural pride, and from the percep-

tion of what is worthy or unworthy of the self, which instinctively asserts itself.

But *why* is it that honor is found in rendering justice rather than injustice, in telling the truth rather than a lie? Why is not pride felt in a deed of robbery or extortion, or a skilful lie, just as much as in honest and truthful behavior? Surely there is quite as much self-assertion in the one class of acts as in the other. It is not, then, merely to the act of self-assertion, as Professor Everett acknowledges, that we give our praise or blame. Professor Everett endeavors, therefore, to analyze it into deeper elements, and makes the honor of self-assertion conditional upon the fulness of the self which is revealed, and upon self-consistency between our word and our conduct, between our passions and our reason, as parts of the self, whose proper relation is overthrown by indulgence in falsehood and vice.

There is a certain measure of truth here, for these are all manifestations, more or less dim, of the primal instincts of the solidarity of life, of the unity of selfhood and of the perfection of personality, in which lie the worth of life and the goal of its evolution. But the deeper and simpler reason is found in that sense of shame which awakens, whenever reason gets its eyes open, in allowing to one's self what one condemns in others. When I find robbery or lying or injustice practised against myself, I resent it, and am indignant at it, as an infringement of my rights. When I am tempted to commit similar transgressions against others, reason bids me put myself in my neighbor's place, and in its impartial mirror discloses the act as equally wrong in myself against another as when committed by that other against myself. So it is with sins of impurity and vice. If in another they rouse disgust or contempt, and we are not willing to grant indulgence in them freely to all, then, in self-consistency, we cannot ourselves indulge in them. We do not have to balance the amount of the self-assertion in a given case over against the amount

18

of its self-sacrifice, nor do we, as the utilitarians would have us think, wait and calculate
what surplus of pleasure over pain, or what
ultimate social advantage, a particular act or
habit may produce, before we pronounce judgment ; but as soon as a reasoning and a
reflecting man, possessed of memory, condemns
a wrong in another, the looking-glass of the
impartial reason shows him where the path of
his own future duty lies. If those we are dealing with are men like ourselves, and we are
members of one social order with them, then
the measure of our obligations toward them is
the same as that of the claims we make or
would make upon them for the security of our
own rights in similar circumstances. This is
the self-consistent rule, the self-evident equation demanded by the impartial reason ; and
therefore it is the moral rule. If we set up
claims for respect for *our* rights, we must in
honor and common-sense respect the equal and
corresponding right of our neighbor ; otherwise, the social structure loses its solidarity

and falls to pieces. And though the unreasoning goose who possesses only sensational sensibility cares only for her own sauce, the goose whose reason becomes at all developed, recognizes that that which is sauce for her is sauce also for the gander.

Thus duty, little by little, becomes completely emancipated from personal limitations and refractions, and stretches outward till it embraces the solidarity of mankind, as a family possessed of equal and God-given rights, and bound · together in universal relations. The moral ideal becomes one of the chief forces in the social environment, moulding the man's sentiments and inclinations, and through them the future conduct of himself and those around. The individual, seeking equilibrium with the forces acting upon himself, finds that the most needed of all adaptations is that which adapts his own conduct to his own idea of what it should be. With irresistible force the science of ethics is carried onward and upward till it becomes the science of complete manhood; and we see that our manhood is but a severed and dying branch unless it recognizes the equal rights of every other fellow-limb of the great tree of humanity.

CHAPTER X.

THIS power of the moral ideal to incarnate itself is a power which the moralist should not overlook. Especially, in reference to that noblest of duties, the duty of self-sacrifice for others, should it be given a large sphere of influence.

Mr. Spencer's system has no proper justification to furnish for this ideal. When the patriot dies for his country, when the apostle of scientific and religious liberty renders himself a willing object of persecution or death for the grand cause of truth, it is an act which his fellow-countrymen will naturally praise, because they reap the benefit of it; it is an act of glorious madness, to which the demoniac power of ancient superstition or hereditary awe of authority hurried the poor man: but it was not, in the view of the new ethics, an act commanded by any authority or endowed with any legitimate sanction. He who understands the kind of psychological metamorphic rock that habit, custom, despotism, ancient priesthoods, and modern enthusiasms can produce, will understand just how much and just how little there is in such a deed.

The trouble again, here, is that Mr. Spencer forgets the dynamic character of *ideas*. Our thoughts are not something inert, an echo of our sensations, powerless images of things in the mirror of the mind, but they are forces that are always exerting a pressure toward action. " In the unintelligent creature," as M. Fouillée well points out,[1] "Nature has to intercalate the motor of sensible pleasure between perception and action ; but in the intelligent being, this middle term of sensible pleasure is no longer necessary, and the mental current takes a more direct course. Ideas point directly to self-expression in corresponding acts." Every psychologist knows how potent is the influence of expectant attention, not only over

[1] Revue des Deux Mondes, 1 Juillet, 1880, p. 130.

enjoyment and bodily health, but also over our very perceptions and our conscious and unconscious motions. He knows how imperative, how tyrannical, a fixed idea is in determining the conduct of a monomaniac. And even with men whom we call perfectly sane, we all know how surely the pet notion which he gets "on the brain," as the saying is, constantly crops out in his daily action. And one of the most interesting tasks of the historian is to trace the manner in which some social dream or philosophic theory or political abstraction of one generation of men becomes an electric bath in which the institutions, governments, churches, and moral life of the next generation are crystallized into forms which they hold for long centuries thereafter. Our moral ideas, especially, draw us by the magnetism of their own nobility and beauty to realize their own high laws in some act of incorruptible justice or self-denying devotion. As beauty is its own excuse for being, so the divine grace and sacredness of these elevated ethical conceptions are the only justification, the only motive power, which they need to explain their objectification in some correlative deed. Wherever a moral ideal has clearly defined itself on the horizon of thought of any human society, there morality has already begun its career, and the tides of a new common life will soon testify to its attraction. The ethical ideas of to-day constitute the environing atmosphere which descends upon us in the dew or hail of to-morrow. As long as man is a thinking being, his thoughts of the true, the just, and the right will be the most decisive elements that condition the growth of customs and institutions.

WHAT is the source of the authority of the moral law? How do we gain our knowledge of the right? In Mr. Spencer's view, the authority and sanction of the great laws of right lie in their greater conduciveness to the general welfare. The feeling of moral obligation he derives, as we have seen, from the particular varieties of re-representative feelings by a process of abstraction of their general quality. "Accumulated experiences have produced the consciousness that the guidance by feelings which refer to remote and general results is *usually more* conducive to welfare than guidance by feelings to be immediately gratified. . . . The idea of authoritativeness has therefore come to be connected with feelings having these traits [remote, complex, re-representative]; the implication being that the lower and simpler feelings are without authority." [1]

But such considerations of expediency can only prescribe the line of prudence; they cannot furnish that binding power which we feel wherever we recognize our duty. To abstract the idea of obligation from that of general welfare, is as impossible as to extract gold from lead, as the alchemists claimed to do. And if the process seems to succeed, it is because the more precious metal is slyly slipped in during the process. The two ideas are ideas of different order. The notion of right is one that is undecomposable and unique. It declares the debt which is owed by us, as a member of society, to that whole of which we are a part. It shows the ideal which, un-realized, reproaches us with its culpable dis-cord. It pronounces, not what is or may be, but what must be; and if cold facts oppose it, it retorts, " So much the worse for the facts." Though justice and truth be found nowhere on

[1] Data of Ethics, p. 126.

the earth, their ideal worth and authority over our future efforts are none the less binding. And that worth and that authority is of a value superior to that of either individual happiness or general welfare. The injustice on which a comfortable majority fattens is none the less an iniquity before the tribunal of righteousness.

There are situations easily conceivable in which all harvest of pleasure in virtue is out of the question, yet in which the heart of man, even of the most inveterate utilitarian, affirms a higher claim. Was it not John Stuart Mill himself, who, in his protest against the immorality of being forced to call a being good who was not at all such a being as that word properly and customarily indicates, nobly declared that if such a being should doom him to eternal hell for refusing him such life-homage, then he would gladly go to that hell rather than to the heaven of such a God?[1] And in one of Professor Huxley's

[1] Examination of Sir W. Hamilton's Philosophy, chap. vii.

well-known addresses there occurs a similar
exalted declaration of loyalty to the right
and true as superior in their claims upon
a true man to any considerations of general
welfare or even the total destruction of all
mankind. "Suppose theology established the
existence of an evil deity (and some theo-
logians, even Christian ones, have come very
near this), is the religious affection to be trans-
ferred from the ethical ideal to any such
omnipotent demon? I trow not. Better a
thousand times that the human race should
perish under his thunderbolts than that it
should say, 'Evil, be thou my good!'" [1]

These are the instinctive sentiments of every
heart that has discerned the sanctity of the
moral ideal, and plainly exhibit its superiority
to all questions of utility or surplus of pleasure;
for if right and wrong are to be measured by
such standards, the destruction of the human
race or the eternal misery of the soul must,
however brought about, be the worst of evils,

[1] Critiques and Addresses, p. 49.

and any device would be right that would
escape them. But even when confronted with
this most terrible of oppressions, the conscience
recognizes a higher bond. As Robert Browning
says, —

> "Justice, good, and truth were still
>   Divine if, by some demon's will,
>   Hatred and wrong had been proclaimed
>   Law through the worlds, and right misnamed." [1]

And this involuntary, unquestioning recognition by every noble nature of the unbought
sovereignty of the moral law plainly exhibits
its eternal and inherent authority and its
independent source. The seat of the moral
law is in no earthly force or institution or
human tribunal, but in "the bosom of God."
It is not because he is All-mighty, but because
he is All-holy and All-good, that we revere
him as divine. The infinite world-organism is
the body and manifestation of God; the laws
of that whole are the eternal laws of God.
And when we recognize the solidarity of our

[1] Christmas Eve, xvii.

vital being with this divine life and embodiment, we begin to see into the heart of the mystery, the unquestionable authority and supreme sanction of duty. Our moral intuitions are simply the unchanging laws of the universe that have emerged to consciousness in the human heart. Under the reiterated impressions of the world-life in which we are environed, and with the clarified vision of truth that is given where the impartial mind begins to look out on the world, the inherent principles of the Universal Reason reflect themselves in the mirror of the moral nature.

CHAPTER XII.

THESE ethical intuitions of humanity are facts, and they are our earliest guides and our court of last resort in all matters of morals. But we should remember that they declare only the simple normal relations of motives and of agents. They assert the solemn distinction that exists between right and wrong; they assert the authority of that right and the aversion and avoidance which should be given to the wrong. Their moral light discloses the worth and lawful claim upon our obedience of the higher motives of truth, love, and purity, and in general of whatever purpose or ideal we see to be nobler and higher than the more animal or selfish impulse that competes with it for our preference. But this moral intuition does not extend, of course, to those complex and distant deductions from these simple principles which form the subject of questions of casuistry, and by which the existence of any moral intuition at all is supposed to be demolished. Place any simple question of the rightfulness or wrongfulness of motives before any conscience that has its moral eyes open, and it will be solved substantially in the same way. The cases where those diversities of judgment arise that are made a constant reproach to intuitive ethics are where there are conflicts of motives and principles, complex and far-extended applications to be made, peculiar circumstances, conditions, and environments to be considered, and especially where the question raised is not one of the *motive* that should rule, but of the outward conduct in which that motive may most usefully embody itself. To expect such questions to be decided by intuitive moral perception is as absurd as to expect the intuitive perceptions on which arithmetic and geometry are founded to decide on the instant, without error, what

is the square root of twenty-three million, or
what relation the contents of a cube bear to
that of a sphere of equal diameter. No one
can tell such things intuitively. And this does
not militate at all against the existence of the
arithmetical and geometric intuitions on which
these sciences are based. In his presentation
of the theory of morals in his "Data of Ethics,"
Mr. Spencer vouchsafes only small authority
to the *à priori* moral truths. They are con-
venient rules of thumb, to save us, in practical
life, from the trouble of always making our
calculation of the surplus of pleasure for ourselves. They express, not eternal truths, but
merely the net result of the moral experience
and conclusions of our ancestors, and a long
series of political, social, and ecclesiastical
restraints consolidated and transformed by
heredity, and so are entitled to a certain pre-
sumption ; but the supremacy of the higher
moral sentiments over our lower sensations
and desires is only "a qualified supremacy,"
and our innate perceptions of right must be

19

"duly enlightened and made precise by an analytic intelligence." [1]

But when Mr. Spencer descends from the thin air of ethical theory to give us his own personal convictions in connection with practical moral questions of the day, he involuntarily discloses a far higher estimate of the moral intuitions. In his article on "Absolute Political Ethics," [2] for example, he does not hesitate to maintain that "there are *à priori* truths which admit of being known by contemplation of the conditions; axiomatic truths which bear to ethics a relation analogous to that which the mathematical axioms bear to the exact sciences." Such axiomatic truths, he claims, are that "when like-natured beings are associated, the required activities must be mutually limited; and that the highest life can result only when the associated beings are so constituted as severally to keep within the required limits."

[1] Data of Ethics, p. 173.
[2] Popular Science Monthly, March, 1890.

Now, if these truths may properly be claimed as moral axioms, surely the many equally simple moral judgments which intuitive moralists have presented may also be admitted as *à priori*. Of course it is not meant, as Mr. Spencer, in this very passage, cautions the reader, that these axiomatic truths are cognizable by all. " For the apprehension of them " (to quote Mr. Spencer's own most wise admonition), " as for the apprehension of similar axioms, a certain mental growth and a certain mental discipline are needed." As a ploughboy cannot form a conception of the axiom that action and reaction are equal and opposite, so is it with these *à priori* ethical truths. But none the less do they bring with themselves, to all who are able to see their necessary truth, their own sufficient evidence.

CHAPTER XIII.

THE chief objections to the authority of these intuitive ethical truths are drawn from the diverse judgments which the conscience of man, it is alleged, has given in different ages and different quarters of the globe. It is indisputable that such diverse moral judgments have existed and still exist. But the assumption that they really deprive intuitive morality of all authority is a fallacious one. It arises chiefly from the great confusion which hangs over the word "conscience." Let us therefore take a page or two to disentangle the misapprehensions which are so popular on this topic.

The word "conscience" stands in general for the moral action of consciousness, and covers, therefore, several radically different activities of the soul. Under the functions of conscience are usually included, —

1. The moral sense, or the perception of a solemn distinction between right and wrong and between our higher and nobler and more spiritual motives on the one hand, and our lower and more animal motives on the other hand.

2. Our feeling of obligation to do the right and to avoid the wrong ; to choose the higher and nobler motive in preference to the lower.

3. The inward witness or self-cognitive activity, which appears when our consciousness, by introspection, compares the lower and higher motives that compete for our approval, and observes which are higher, which are lower ; which our will chooses, and whether or not our choice and subsequent action correspond with our moral knowledge or ethical ideal.

4. The counsellor of conduct, — the judgment, *i. e.*, which prescribes for us befitting acts by which to manifest the motives that the moral cognition has approved, and the moral will decided to follow.

Now, it is only in the realm of the first two —

in perceiving the distinction between right and wrong, and the obligation to obey the right and avoid the wrong, and in certain elementary moral judgments of certain motives as nobler, and therefore preferable, to certain others — that moral intuition, properly speaking, is to be recognized. The third field is a domain sometimes called intuitive, because it is a domain of direct interior sight; but to be precise, it should rather be called the *introspective* field of conscience. It does not declare the eternal and the immutable laws of morality, but observes the particular facts of our ethical life.

The fourth domain, although often spoken of as a field of moral intuition, is really the province of reason and experience, of deduction and induction. Though popularly we say that conscience bids us not to kill or forge or rob, yet this is not properly the work of conscience, but of the reason, thus to sit in judgment on our acts; and this fourth domain of external conduct is properly not a domain of morals at all, but is only called so by courtesy, because of

its close connection with the moral witness
and sovereign whose wishes it essays to realize in its lower sphere of wise and prudent
administration. It is simply the executive
department attached to the supreme court of
conscience. Now, as this executive arm of conscience (the practical judgment) has to learn by
long and hard experience what are the most expedient methods of carrying out the moral purposes that the man has in view, it is only
natural that in primitive times, in savage
tribes, in the various levels of mental and
moral culture, there should be many diversities and irregularities of conduct, many ethical
mistakes. Even where the conscience is most
acute and the moral culture high, these mistakes occur, because they are really not acts
of the *moral* faculty, but of the reason, conditioned in its action by its experience and opportunities of observation and wise judgment.
Under different circumstances, the same act
will be a wise or an unwise mode of realizing

good motives. And moreover, the same motive, that in comparison with a lower motive had seemed right, when the thoughts of man have risen to entertain higher principles of action will now seem wrong. Take the case of the Fijian instanced by Mr. Spencer, and which he regards as overthrowing the hypothesis that " the wrongness of murder is known by a moral intuition which the human mind was originally constituted to yield." [1] Mr. Spencer here demolishes only a man of straw, not the modern intuitional view of ethics. If the Fijian considers that the slaughter of a member of a neighboring tribe is an honorable thing, it is because he compares the trait of manly bravery and skill which it requires with the lower motives of sloth, cowardice, or other inferior spring of action. It is not because he deliberately compares the violation of his duty to his fellowmen with respect for it, and decides in favor of the first. Still less does it mean that he

[1] Data of Ethics, p. 39.

has no sense of duty at all. It shows only that his sense of duty and honor has not been extended to those outside his own tribe, any more than that of a large part of Christendom has been extended to the brute creation.

CHAPTER XIV.

TO enable a man to conduct himself with wisdom and usefulness amongst his fellow-men, it is necessary that the most favorable social conditions should join hands; and in order that we may bring the higher motives of universal benevolence, honesty, and truth into play, we must, by deeper and wider experiences of life, gain clearer moral insight. It is not strange, then, that man's ethical vision is only gradually opened. The earlier morality of the human race was very crude, and had undoubtedly much dross of fear, selfishness, superstition, and low utilitarianism mingled with it. But because the moral sentiments were originally thus impure and had their origin amidst miry fens, the validity of their testimony is not shown to be invalid and their own sovereignty illusive. Is the grape not to be reckoned sweet, or the rose beau-

tiful, because it started on its career as
a bitter, unsightly bud? Is the lung not to
be trusted as an organ of breathing in the
upper air because embryology shows that it
was in its origin only a swim-bladder in deni-
zens of the water? As Mr. Sidgwick well
says: " No one appeals from the artist's sense
of beauty to the child's, nor are the truths of
the higher mathematics thought to be less certainly true because they can only be appre-
hended by a highly developed intellect. In
fact, this disposition to attribute some strange
importance and special authority to what was
first felt or thought, belongs to an antiquated
point of view. In politics we have quite
abandoned the idea that if we could establish
irrefragably the original condition of the human
family, it would help to determine jural obligations in our existing societies. The corresponding opinion still lingers in psychology and
ethics, but it may be expected to linger not
very long ; as the assumption that our *earliest*
consciousness is most trustworthy is not only

baseless, but opposed to the current theories of evolution and progress."

Social conditions, customs of revenge, political despotisms, and animistic superstitions may all have helped to open our moral eyes, — just as the long and varied experiences of our race have all contributed something toward perfecting our intellectual vision. But because man's logical and mathematic powers have only been very slowly developed and brought up to their present strength by very indirect processes, and there are still savage tribes who cannot count ten, shall we say that we may not legitimately and confidently unite major and minor premises into any conclusion, or that our geometric axioms or mathematical calculations are not to be depended upon ? Because man's physical eyes have been developed from inferior organs of vision and the first rudiment of an eye that appeared on the stage of animal existence was hardly worthy to be called an eye at all, shall we say that the process of perception cannot be trustworthy ? Subjective

idealism, to be sure, doubts the trustworthiness
of all knowledge, because it accepts no objective realities. But it has been the precise
work of modern science and the evolution
philosophy to vindicate the objective reality
of things, and with it the trustworthiness of
our faculties. It has shown that it is because
the ether and the ethereal vibrations first
exist that they have called into existence and
moulded into harmony with them the visual
organ to perceive them. It is because solid
things exist about us in certain relations that
our sense of touch and pressure and our ideas
of space have been evoked. The relations between the outer realities and the inner sensibility evoke the different sensations and mould
the organ to the increased susceptibility that
perceives them more exactly. Further experiences with the relations of extended things
and the development of thought to analyze
those relations and see what they imply, leads
the intellect, when sufficiently developed, to
perceive the properties of squares and circles,

of number and forces. The physical relations in the things perceived by the intellectual vision give rise to the necessary mathematical truths, eternal as the space and matter whose inherent properties they express.

So when social intercourse brings to consciousness the moral forces within man and the moral relations in the midst of which he necessarily lives, and when evolution unfolds our instincts of right and wrong into distinct ethical perceptions and laws, these perceptions and laws are also things to be trusted. The recognition of the long process of development by which our moral nature has been unfolded does not damage its testimony or show its authority to be illusive or its sovereignty merely due to its superior productivity of happiness, but it indorses and corroborates its validity. For in the first place, though evolution, it may be granted, has been the instrumentality which by its long grinding and patient polishing has perfected the lens of conscience, we must recognize the primitive moral crystal as existing from the outset. To change the figure, there must have been a true ethical germ at the start, or this derivation is hopelessly invalidated. The explicitly moral can come only from the implicitly moral, — not from any absolutely unmoral source, any more than existence can come from non-existence. And this moral germ must have been something as unique in its kind as the fully developed conscience. "The greatest of all distinctions in biology when it first arises," says Mr. Romanes, "is thus seen to be in its *potentiality* rather than in its origin. The distinction between a nature that can and a nature which cannot possess moral power, is capital." And however much our sense of the moral worth of the higher feelings and the moral odiousness of the lower may have grown in clearness and delicacy, these moral perceptions are of a distinct order and kind; they are indecomposable into judgments of prudence, and their authority in moral decisions is not due to a surplus of pleasure, but to the discernment of a different kind and quality of motive, — the kind that more becomes a true man. "The moral ought," as Professor Sidgwick [1] admits, "is an ultimate and unanalyzable fact." The consciousness that we have of the superior worth of right is a consciousness unique in its kind, and against which no feeling of pleasure, however great its quantity, is to be balanced, wherever a man's conscience is normally developed.

And a second, equally incontrovertible, equally weighty reason is that right and wrong are not artificial, due to the caprice of chieftain or priest or fashion of the hour, but they are due to the just and befitting relations of man to man, inherent in human nature and in the conditions of existence. The moral forces and conditions precede and mould society and awaken the latent ethical sense just as the magnetic forces group in symmetric forms the iron filings scattered on a paper held over a magnet. The paramount claims of love or truth do not arise from the coer-

[1] See Mind, October, 1889.

cions of social, political, or ecclesiastical institutions, or from experience of more general
and remote utilities associated with them. It
is rather a consciousness due to our recognition of the inherent excellence of these virtuous motives, the sense of our union for good
or evil with our fellows, and the self-consistency in giving to others what we demand
from them, that reason and honor both require.
As our knowledge of man and Nature grows
wider and wider, we find the great principles
of right interwoven with the texture of our
own personality, and we find that web to be
an inseparable part of the great web of human
society. We see that the great principles of
ethics are things that neither fashion nor custom nor statute-book can make or unmake,
but that they are ingrained in the nature of
human existence, — of life itself. They are
eternal conditions of our continuance as social
beings, and therefore they have a claim on
our obedience from which we cannot run
away. In loyalty to this claim men have

wasted away in dungeons, braved the fatal contagion of disease, given up the fairest earthly prospects, to bear witness to the truth or succor the suffering. These self-sacrifices and martyrdoms are only intelligible when we recognize a law of holiness claiming our loyalty and carrying with it its own evidence. And there is a further consideration here pointed out by Professor Green in his able "Prolegomena to Ethics," [1] which it is well to notice. In any case of self-denial this personal sacrifice involves (according to the hedonistic doctrine of good, whether universalistic or egoistic) just so much of a deduction from true good as the amount of the personal pleasure that is lost; and this is justified only when he who meditates this self-denial can see clearly that it will produce a much larger addition of pleasure to the common stock from other quarters. Now, to the one who is called upon for the sacrifice, his own loss is very certain; while the addition

[1] Page 420.

of greater happiness to the common stock, through others' pleasure, is always a more or less uncertain calculation; and where the self-sacrifice is one not usually called for by conventional morality, but by a higher ideal of moral perfection, the calculation of the probability of an increased balance of happiness would rarely be certain enough to justify it. The tendency of the hedonistic theory of ethics is always therefore against self-sacrifice, as a more uncertain means of adding to the common stock of happiness than personal indulgence. Where men determine their acts by such considerations, self-sacrifice will be more often discouraged than encouraged; but if we accept, on the contrary, the realization of the highest capabilities of humanity as our ultimate moral end and standard, then it is evident at once that that exercise of a devoted will which is shown by an act of self-denial is of itself a positive and sure contribution to true moral good. The personal consecration of the spirit which is exhibited by every self-

sacrificing deed has intrinsic moral excellence ;
it is itself a noticeable upward step on the lad-
der of moral perfection and an inspiration of
the most precious kind to all who witness it.
Virtue has a self-propagating power. Heroism and love in any one man never fail to
strengthen the same noble qualities in those
around. A correct idea of the ultimate moral
end thus both justifies and sanctions that
moral heroism which so instinctively we all
admire, and also tends steadily to foster such
nobler manifestations in the field of human
life.

The real reason, then, why man is a moral
being is not to be found in any such secondary
considerations as Mr. Spencer refers us to, —
such as fear of private revenge and dread of
governmental punishment, nor yet in ghostly
superstitions nor ecclesiastical despotisms, nor
all the varied pressures of man's social relations. Whatever these may have contributed,
there is a deeper cause, without which all
these would have been without effect. And

this deeper cause is, first, that man is a part
of a moral universe in which he has grown
up, and by which he has been moulded, and in
which these inherent laws are revealed ; and,
second, that he has a reason capable of dis-
cerning these moral laws, and a consciousness
capable of feeling the inseparable bonds that
bind him to the greater whole of which he is
a member. The Power that manifests itself
in the universe is one that ever makes for
righteousness. Vice and injustice are ever
destroying themselves. In the struggle for
existence the social life and the altruistic
forces steadily gain upon the isolated and
selfish mode of existence. The great world
process is one that yearly brings all the members of humanity into closer union with one
another, and man himself into a broader and
more intimate communion with all other parts
of the universe. This world-process mingles
itself with our personality, and interweaves
itself with us in all moral and spiritual phenomena. Our conscience is rightly understood

only when it is recognized as the voice of the spiritual nature inwoven with our whole personality. And that personality must be looked upon as a part of a grander spiritual whole. Beauty, truth, right, wisdom, are all ideals to which we instinctively reach upward, and which bind us to them by their self-evidencing authority. To bring the varied tendencies of humanity into unity, we must recognize them as attributes of one common life, and refer all our moral impulses to a great Moral Power, of which they are the manifestations and effects.

We may look upon the moral laws, therefore, as the vital reactions of the plastic organization of humanity to the constantly repeated impressions of the righteous Cosmic Life in which man is environed, emerging at length in human consciousness in the forms of intuitions of duty and the rightful supremacy of the higher motives over the lower; and the enlightened conscience we may regard as the expression in the human soul of the Divine Consciousness. Our higher aspirations have such spontaneous authority because they are the revelation of our deepest needs and most essential nature, the prophetic voice of that destiny of which we are still for the most part unconscious. Morality is the victory of the Divine Life in us, — " the inward sovereign spirit of the universe that has ever moved onward from chaos to cosmos, from lifelessness to life, from the outward to the inward." The objective foundation of ethics is in that Unity of the All which secures the unchanging orderliness of events and which binds all the parts of the Universe and the members of its great household into one interdependent whole. The superior value of a right action is due to the fact that it is a part of that great tide which sweeps through eternity, and through which the stars are kept in their orbit and " the most ancient heavens are fresh and strong." That same universal order of things that makes mathematics, geometry, and logic possible, also furnishes ethics with its invulnerable basis. And it is the instinc-

tive feeling of this vital and eternal solidarity
of our life with the universal life, emerging
from unconsciousness to consciousness, which
gives our sense of obligation its unconditional
sacredness and transcendent authority.   The
cautious Mr. Sidgwick has put it on record
that he " is not prepared to deny that the conception of duty carries with it the implied
relations of our individual will with an Universal will." [1]   And if the wariest and severest
of ethical critics finds such probability in this
view, both they to whom the intuitions of the
spirit are not condemned in advance as mere
hallucinations, and they who carefully seek for
the most rational explanation of this mystic,
yet undeniable constraint of moral obligation,
may gladly adopt this higher view.

The work of a moral being is, then, the voluntary bringing of his personal will into harmony
and co-operation with this supreme Will which
moves through all.   The holy life is that in

[1] Sidgwick, 3d ed., p. 216.

which the human spirit is placed *en rapport*
with the Divine Spirit. As a member of the
great macrocosm, the human microcosm must
regulate his individual conduct and purposes
by the grander object of the whole. In the
instinctive tendencies and organized impulses
of human nature we have valuable revelations
of these cosmic plans and divine laws; but
these disclosures are only partial, and more or
less alloyed with the carnal dross of our animal
heritage. It is by the light of reason that we
discern the universal laws of righteousness and
the eternal conditions of associated existence.
Reason is therefore the essential subjective
factor in ethics, as the unity of the individual
with the universal life is the prime objective
factor. We see this cosmic organism moving
upward on the path of evolution toward perfection, and we recognize in the impulse that
constantly spurs us to improve ourselves and
the world about us, the inspiration of the universal spirit of progress. This aspiration for

perfection becomes the moral law of man's life; and as his experience broadens, he constantly enlarges his ideas and desire for good to a more all-embracing circumference. The true aim of human life (which is therefore also the true standard of morals) is recognized to be nothing less than the closest possible approximation we can achieve to such a moral and intellectual perfection as is exhibited in the Being from whom man emanates. The test of the rightfulness of any act is its tendency to exalt and complete the spiritual development of our race. That act is wrong which tends in the opposite direction. Evolution from the lower to the higher, from the carnal to the spiritual, is not merely the path of man's past pilgrimage, but the destiny to which the future calls him; for it is the path which brings his spirit into closest resemblance to the World-Essence and most intimate union with it. That instinct for the betterment of our life, which in its lowest forms is the condition of even successful animal existence, and which in its highest form aspires to infinite perfection, is of the very essence of humanity ; for it is the abiding witness in man of the Infinite Spirit who is ever educing higher from lower, and better from worse, in endless progression, and in whose unending Life we all " live and move and have our being."

FINIS.

STORIES OF THE SEEN AND THE UNSEEN.

BY

Mrs. MARGARET O. W. OLIPHANT.

This volume includes the four books hitherto published anonymously, viz.: "A Little Pilgrim: In the Unseen;" "The Little Pilgrim: Further Experiences, etc.;" "Old Lady Mary, a Story of the Seen and the Unseen;" "The Open Door. The Portrait: Two Stories of the Seen and the Unseen."

One volume. 16mo. Cloth. Price, $1.25.

——◆——

As bits of imaginative writing, Mrs. Oliphant's "Stories of the Seen and the Unseen" are exquisite productions. The experience of the Little Pilgrim on her waking in heaven, and her return to earth with her soul filled with the light of a Divine beneficence and her mind sure of those higher truths, to soothe earthly sufferers revolting against the bitterness of loss and pain, are told with the sublimated spirituality of one who has just passed through a long illness, and whose mind, weak to the impressions of the external world, is peculiarly sensitive to spiritual visions. No one could have written with more poetic delicacy of the subjective and objective blessedness of that state of future existence which the human heart pictures to itself by the word heaven; and the story of "Old Lady Mary" will remain a distinct success among tales of imaginative literature. — *The Critic.*

We commend the literary delicacy and power of these stories, and even more their tender, stimulating spirituality. — *Congregationalist.*

Deep spiritual truths are given a new beauty; the idea of Divine love and beneficence is never lost sight of, and the heart that is filled with sorrow will find in the story of the Little Pilgrim a soothing charm and a something that may heal the scars which have been made by grief and bereavement. — *Philadelphia Record.*

——◆——

For sale by all booksellers. Mailed, post-paid, on receipt of price, by the publishers,

ROBERTS BROTHERS, Boston.

HISTORY OF THE PEOPLE OF ISRAEL.

By ERNEST RENAN,

AUTHOR OF "LIFE OF JESUS."

VOL. I. — TILL THE TIME OF KING DAVID.

VOL. II. — FROM THE REIGN OF DAVID UP TO THE CAPTURE OF SAMARIA.

VOL. III. — FROM THE TIME OF HEZEKIAH TILL THE RETURN FROM BABYLON.

8vo. Cloth. Price, $2.50 per volume.

———◆———

It may safely be predicted that Renan's latest production will take rank as his most important since the "Life of Jesus." There is the same charming style, the same brilliancy of treatment, the same clear judgment and delicate touches, the deep thoughts and thorough mastery of his subject, which have made Renan one of the most fascinating of modern writers. — *New York Times.*

To all who know anything of M. Renan's "Life of Jesus" it will be no surprise that the same writer has told the "History of the People of Israel till the Time of King David" as it was never told before nor is ever like to be told again. For but once in centuries does a Renan arise, and to any other hand this work were impossible. Throughout it is the perfection of paradox, for, dealing wholly with what we are all taught to lisp at the mother's knee, it is more original than the wildest romance ; more heterodox than heterodoxy, it is yet full of large and tender reverence for that supreme religion that brightens all time as it transcends all creeds. — *The Commercial Advertiser.*

Many are the histories of Israel. Among them M. Renan's is absolutely unique, though it has traits in common with the most diverse of them, — methods and results in common with Ewald and Kuenen and Wellhausen and Stade, beauty of style in common with Milman and Stanley. But the beauty of his style is not the beauty of theirs. It is something far more exquisite. More perfect in its delicate grace it could not be. . . . M. Renan is much more than a critic, much more than a historian. He is a creative literary artist. . . . It is hardly necessary to say that, incidental to the principal contention of his book, M. Renan has many just and admirable observations on the Old Testament literature, and on particular events. Moreover, his general reflections, though often cynical, are always bright and keen, and have frequently a serious and penetrative excellence. — *Am. Unitarian Review.*

———◆———

Sold by all booksellers. Mailed, post-paid, on receipt of price, by the publishers,

ROBERTS BROTHERS, BOSTON.

ETHICAL RELIGION.

BY WILLIAM MACKINTIRE SALTER.

One volume. 12mo. Cloth, Price, $1.50.

The familiar saying about the prophet and his own country is freshly illustrated by Mr. William M. Salter, of the Chicago Society for Ethical Culture, whose works might be called for in vain at most American bookstores, and which are yet translated into German, and in Germany everywhere, as Mr. Edwin D. Mead writes, exposed for sale. . . . We, for our part, will say that the compliment done Mr. Salter in the recognition of his earnest and thoughtful work is richly deserved. — *Chicago Dial.*

He [Mr. Salter] is a man of eloquence and earnestness, as these discourses show ; and their translation into German evinces their power to commend themselves to a much wider constituency than that to which they were first addressed. — *The American.*

There is not a little to commend in this volume. It inculcates a lofty morality, and is far above the level of the utilitarian and evolutionary moralists. — *Presbyterian Review.*

I am particularly obliged to you for Salter's book. Please say to him that I feel that I have gained theoretically as well as practically from reading it. What a noble and pure spirit breathes through the whole! I have derived a fresh confidence in the power of a philosophy of life based on free investigation. — *Professor Harold Höffding, of the University of Copenhagen.*

In the *Zeitschrift für Philosophie und Philosophische Kritik* (*Beigabeheft des 89 sten Bandes*, 1886) Professor Jodl says, at the conclusion of an extended review : —

To a book like Strauss's *Old and New Faith* is *Die Religion der Moral* for these reasons infinitely superior, as well with respect to its scientific foundation as to its practical influence; and I cannot omit to recommend Salter's book to the most earnest attention of all those who feel the need of replacing the unhappy dualism between the religious and the scientific stand-points with a comprehensive ideal view.

Sold by all booksellers. Mailed, post-paid, on receipt of price, by the publishers.

ROBERTS BROTHERS, BOSTON.

IN HIS NAME.

A Story of the Waldenses, Seven Hundred Years Ago.

Illustrated.

By EDWARD E. HALE.

16mo, cloth, 129 illustrations by G. P. JACOMB-HOOD.

PRICE, $1.25.

It deals with the Waldenses, reads like a troubadour song, as the late Mrs. Jackson said, and fully deserves the holiday dress in which it is now brought out. The book will delight all readers who understand integrity, purity, and good-sense: it is historically accurate; it is a jewel, both as a work of art and in ethics; and it is good holiday reading. — *Beacon.*

ROBERTS BROTHERS . . . BOSTON.